CW01149523

Fate Intertwined

Aparna Samala

INDIA • SINGAPORE • MALAYSIA

Copyright © Aparna Samala 2024
All Rights Reserved.
ISBN
Hardcase 9798896105367
Paperback 9798896105350

This book has been published with all efforts taken to make the material error-free after the consent of the author. However, the author and the publisher do not assume and hereby disclaim any liability to any party for any loss, damage, or disruption caused by errors or omissions, whether such errors or omissions result from negligence, accident, or any other cause.

While every effort has been made to avoid any mistake or omission, this publication is being sold on the condition and understanding that neither the author nor the publishers or printers would be liable in any manner to any person by reason of any mistake or omission in this publication or for any action taken or omitted to be taken or advice rendered or accepted on the basis of this work. For any defect in printing or binding the publishers will be liable only to replace the defective copy by another copy of this work then available.

DEDICATION

To the woman who has been my guiding star, my unwavering source of support, and my greatest champion throughout my life, I dedicate this book.

My dearest mum Amma, you have consistently been the wind beneath my wings, propelling me to reach for the stars and embrace my passion for writing. It is your faith in me and your wish to see what happens next that made me write this book.

This book stands as a testament to the countless times you've said, 'Just keep writing more and follow your heart wherever it leads you.'

So, Amma, with immense love and gratitude, this book is dedicated to you.

Thank you for being my rock, my guiding light, and the reason I continue to put pen to paper.

With all my love and deepest gratitude,
Aparna

CONTENTS

Preface 7

Foreword 11

Acknowledgements 13

Prologue 15

Chapter 1   A Day to Look Back To 19

Chapter 2   Disha in Goa 35

Chapter 3   Arjun 45

Chapter 4   Asha, My First Love 53

Chapter 5   Our First Valentine's Day 65

Chapter 6   Finding Our Passions 77

Chapter 7   That Fateful Day 87

Chapter 8   Exploring the City Together 107

Chapter 9   The Beginning of a New Chapter 113

Chapter 10   Hidden Desires 119

Chapter 11   Doubts and Challenges 129

Chapter 12   With the Girls 135

৯০ Contents ৫৪

Chapter 13	Getting Back Home	143
Chapter 14	A Pact to Face Uncertainties	153
Chapter 15	Becoming Each Other's Rock	163
Chapter 16	A Lifetime of Love	175

Afterword and Additional Insights 181

PREFACE

As Varun and Disha meet each other after a decade, Disha feels a sense of panic throughout. Her first response to seeing Varun was flight. Then she pauses and decides to face the ends up facing the truth and realises that she got her closure long back, and somehow seeing Varun after a long time makes her realise that she doesn't have any questions to ask him, as the answers are futile now. They part ways officially, making closure to their unrequited love story. The second innings in each of their lives begin with Arjun entering Disha's life and Varun going ahead with his life and ambitions.

Fate Intertwined is the story of how small incidents play a bigger role in bringing two people together and driving them apart. There is no way you can understand what is going on, let alone know what to do. It is only in hindsight that you will realise that it happened for a particular reason and to redirect you to your destiny. Many times, you are left wondering, what if I chose a different option? If we keep thinking back, there is no end to it. Our past is only a measure to course-correct our future.

"Fate Intertwined" is not merely a love story; it is a journey into the heart of what it means to find someone who doesn't try to change your world but becomes part of it. It delves

Preface

into how deep connections can form in the least expected ways and how these connections can withstand the tests of time, distance, and circumstances.

The characters you will meet, whose lives unfold in these pages, were crafted from a blend of observation and imagination. They embody the spirit of real human emotion—flawed, perfect, and everything in between. Through them, I wish to convey that in every moment of weakness, there is potential for strength, and in every instance of despair, there is a possibility for hope.

This story began as a whisper of thought, a what-if that spiralled into the narrative before you. It was written for those who wanted to know what happened next in Disha's life. It is for those who felt twisted in love and feel it changed their world. For those who were hurt and wanted to heal and for those who were confused in a relationship. Remember one thing: being in love should never be confusing. Life is not about filling it with What ifs; it is about the paths chosen. This story is for those who have braved the vulnerability of love and have been hurt. It is for those who feel that they have lost everything to that one person who doesn't have the same wavelength. It is for those who have been pouring all their energy into others broken vessel while got nothing in return other than the despair and for those who kept wondering if there is something wrong within them. It is for every heart that has felt the deep-seated yearning for connection.

Preface

"Fate Intertwined" is a testament to the belief that, no matter how tangled our lives may seem, love has the power to align us with our destined paths.

FOREWORD

Many of my friends who read the first book, *Seamless Thoughts*, were curious about what would happen next. As Shahrukh Khan says in one of his movies, "Picture abhi baaki hain, mere dost," till there is "The End," card, the show must go on. The same is the case with Disha.

Fate, I believe, brings the right people into your life when you need them and lets them go when they no longer serve the purpose. Let me take you on the tour with Disha to see how her journey goes after bidding goodbye to Varun.

Within the pages of this book, you will encounter characters who are both ordinary and extraordinary, their lives bound by a common thread—fate. As their stories unfold, you will witness the ripple effects of their choices, the unforeseen consequences of their actions, and the beautiful encounters that forever alter the course of their lives. Through their experiences, we are reminded that our own lives are similarly intertwined with the lives of others, creating a rich amalgamation of shared moments, joys, and sorrows.

This book is an invitation to ponder the intricate dance of fate and free will, to glimpse the beauty that emerges when destinies intersect, and to find solace in the idea that, in the end, our lives are woven into a magnificent menagerie that is greater than the sum of its individual threads. As you embark

Foreword

on this journey, may you discover the profound connections that bind us all and the enduring power of human agency in shaping our own stories.

Let us explore the boundless mysteries of "Fate Intertwined" together.

ACKNOWLEDGEMENTS

To my parents, who have been with me in every step of my life, silently protecting me from the unwanted disruptions of the world. Without their guidance, I am nothing. I am forever indebted to them for what and who I am. Thank you, amma and baba.

My sisters, who are always watching over me and guiding me through their lives, help me course-correct my thoughts. Thank you, darlings.

My brother, who knows exactly what he wants and who, in his own way, has taught me to prioritise myself over everything else. I found my voice and my stance by watching him take his. Thank you, bro, for guiding me to make my space a precious one and standing beside me, letting me do my own things.

My lovely kid, who is the most adorable one on earth and has a lot of patience for my tantrums. All he needs is some chit-chat time. Love you so much, and according to him, I am the bestest mum in the whole wide world (of course, there is no word called "bestest" but you get the depth of it). Those words bring a smile every single time, and his hugs make me feel that I am precious to my darling. Thank you, baby, for being the most obedient kid in the "whole wide world." Lots of love.

ॐ Acknowledgements ☙

Last but not least, my friends who read my first book were eager and encouraged me to write more. I am glad to have been bestowed upon by such beautiful souls who help me in their own way.

PROLOGUE

In the vibrant heart of Mumbai, where the city's relentless energy met the dreams of countless souls, there lived a woman named Disha. She is a combination of brilliance and strength, a solitary woman venturing on a path of love and self-exploration like any other.

Disha's intelligence was matched only by her boundless talent. She had a way of lighting up a room with her presence, her laughter contagious, and her smile a beacon of hope. Yet, beneath her radiant exterior lay a story of strength and resilience that had been forged in the crucible of life's most challenging trials.

Disha had made a choice that would forever shape the course of her life. She had opened her heart and home to a young girl, a child who had needed love and nurturing more than anything else. It was a decision born of pure love and a desire to live on while her heart was broken.

Before the journey into motherhood could truly begin, Disha had navigated the heart-wrenching landscape of love. She had experienced an overwhelming passion that felt like it could engulf her entirely, a bond that pledged eternity but faded away like a fleeting reverie. The person who had once held her entire world had disappeared with

Prologue

no trace. She had been ghosted by the one who had once meant the world to her, leaving behind a void that seemed impossible to fill.

The aftermath of heartbreak had taken her through the treacherous layers of depression. It was a darkness that threatened to suffocate her spirit, an abyss from which escape seemed impossible. Yet, in the depths of despair, Disha found a wellspring of strength within herself that she had never known existed. She emerged from the shadows, not merely surviving but thriving, her spirit tempered, and her wisdom deepened.

Through every twist and turn, Disha was not alone. She had a circle of fierce and loyal friends, a gang of girls who were not just friends but her chosen family. In times of trouble, they were her pillars of support, offering unwavering love, laughter, and the warmth of belonging.

Then, a chapter of her life began to unfold against the backdrop of Goa's sun-kissed beaches and the playful dance of the waves. In this picturesque paradise, Disha's path converged with a man named Arjun. Their meeting, like so many moments in life, was a convergence of chance and destiny, or was it Fate Intertwined?

Arjun was an enigma, a man with his own secrets and stories, a man who would either become a part of Disha's future or be yet another lesson in the unpredictable journey of life.

Prologue

As we embark on this journey with Disha, we are left with the question: Will Arjun be the missing piece in the intricate puzzle of her life, or will he deliver another lesson that fate has in store? Only time will tell as the pages of destiny turn and the story of Disha unfolds.

CHAPTER 1

A DAY TO LOOK BACK TO

I came rushing to my room, feeling pretty flustered. I almost had a mini heart attack out there.

My phone started ringing, snapping me back to reality. It's Ananya.

"Hey, mum, what are you up to? You didn't call me this morning. Where is my good morning kiss and a hug? Do I need to ask you that? I miss you so much..." Ananya went on and on.

I chuckled and said, "Slow down, sweetheart. How are you doing? Lots of love and kisses to you. I miss you too, but I think I will come back after a few days. I will be staying back a week here in Goa."

"What, no, why, mum? What is going on? Is everything okay with you? Are you hurt? Shall I call Gayathri aunty?" Ananya got worried.

"Nothing to worry, baby. I want to explore the place more. I need a break from my routine. Is it okay if I stay back more?" I asked.

"Of course, mum. I am a big girl. I can take care of myself and Granny, too," she said.

I put the phone down and started to wonder, what came upon me? Wow, I just made an impulsive decision. I want to explore. I got scared. I think it is time to call my besties. I messaged them.

"Girls..."

Gayatri was the first to ping back.

"What the hell... we told you to stay away from us and take a break. You were not supposed to message and have a fun time. Why on earth are you pinging us early in the morning?"

"Something happened," I said.

"Are you ok?" Nisha asked.

"I met Varun," I said.

"Get on to a video call right now," Gayatri said, and the rest followed.

There was total silence.

"Babes, do you want us there? Are you okay? Do you want to come back? Please don't go back to that danger zone again," Gayathri started saying, looking all concerned and worried.

"Please calm down and don't put such worried faces. I am all fine, and I am glad I met him," I said.

"What?" Nisha said.

"Well, yeah. I got pretty scared as soon as I saw him. I had goosebumps all over me. I met him at the airport. I got so scared that I ran away into the washroom. I was just hoping that he would leave. Then I got into the plane, and voila, he came there and sat right next to me."

"You've got to be kidding," screamed Nisha.

"Listen to the full story, naa," I said, smiling.

"She is smiling; something is seriously wrong. Have you gone mad? Don't you remember how much you have suffered because of that asshole? I know he was your first and only love or something, but still. He didn't even turn back once. He didn't care if you existed, and now he suddenly turns up, and you are all smiling. I feel like coming there and smacking that face of yours. Have you forgotten everything?" Gayathri said angrily.

She has the right to be angry. There were countless days when I hugged her and cried like a baby. I was a lost soul. She put up with me so much and was right behind me in every step. I am alive thanks to her. She got Ananya into my life. She made my life meaningful.

"Ufff... Gayathri, Listen please. Don't get all rattled up. Just listen, ok," I said.

"Fine, tell me..." Gayathri said.

"Well, where was I? Yeah, he came and sat next to me, and I got really scared. I didn't know what to do. He tried to talk to me, and I just didn't want to talk to him as I knew that I might either blast at him or cry. I was not prepared for the scenario. I just wanted to get up and run back home. I felt weak in the knees and was almost shivering, so I acted calmly, said I was sleepy, and closed my eyes. I could sense him watching me. I didn't know what else to do. I was super scared to even open my eyes. So, for the whole flight, I just kept my eyes closed. I was damn worried that the tears would fall from my eyes, and he would know that I was still hurting. I just kept praying that he would look away and leave so that I don't have to talk to him."

"Poor you. It must have been terrible. I knew it was a bad idea to send you out alone. Gayathri, see what you did," Nisha said.

"Actually, that's the best thing you gals did," I exclaimed with a sense of gratitude in my voice. "I faced my fears head-on. Gayathri, before I forget, this is the best gift ever. You won't believe how at ease I am now. Let me finish the story first, though."

So, there I was; the plane had just landed, and I could feel his gaze locked on me. Without saying a word, I made my way off the plane. It was getting close to midnight, and I must admit I was feeling a bit uneasy. The thought of travelling alone in a cab for nearly an hour and a half at that hour in midnight in a new place sent shivers down my spine. As I stood there, a bit on edge, Varun asked if I was okay with him joining me. I didn't respond immediately, but deep down, I was relieved. You see, the cab driver seemed a bit off, and I wasn't in the mood for any challenges at that moment. I was on edge, to say the least. So, I silently agreed, and he came along.

He attempted to strike up a conversation, but just as he was about to do so, Ananya called me. I spoke with her for a while, and the next thing I knew, I was dozing off in the cab. As we finally reached our destination, he gently woke me up. I felt a tad embarrassed but didn't let it show. He accompanied me as we entered the hotel. After I had checked in, I overheard him asking the receptionist if there were any available rooms. That's when it dawned on me that he hadn't planned on coming to Goa but must have taken a detour after spotting me.

The receptionist informed him that there were no rooms available at the moment and that there would be one ready in the morning. He looked exhausted, and without much hesitation, I offered, "It's okay, you can stay with me for the night." I promptly requested the receptionist to arrange for an extra bed in my room.

"Now, I am sure you have totally gone crazy. Who will let someone who hurt them get into the same room?" Gayathri asked, her voice laced with disbelief.

"Did you guys make out?" came an instant question from Nisha.

"Really, did you?" screamed Shriya.

"Oh my god, either you let me tell you the story, or you can let your imagination go wild," I retorted.

"Okay, okay, fine… Tell us," asked Nisha, her curiosity piqued.

As we entered the room, an undeniable tension hung in the air. The situation was peculiar; we were two people with a shared past, now sharing a room after a decade of silence and separation.

In the room, I couldn't help but notice the shift in dynamics. We weren't the same people we once were. Time had passed, and life had moulded us into different versions of ourselves. Yet, the familiarity lingered like a bittersweet memory.

I sneaked a peek at him. He seems to have aged well. His body was muscular, and the Jaw line was as sharp as before. The eyes seemed genuinely tired, and I couldn't find it in me to hold onto any resentment. He had come all this way, unplanned, just to ensure my safety. In the midst of the silent acknowledgement of our changed circumstances, I watched as he settled onto the extra bed, exhaustion written all over his face.

I simply asked him to freshen up, and he went ahead. Later, I took my own sweet time to freshen up and then came out, said good night, and proceeded to sleep. He fell asleep after some time and looked just like a kid in his slumber. But here's the thing: I couldn't sleep. I kept thinking about all that had happened and all those memories that were locked inside me.

As I lay there in my bed, my thoughts were racing. A few tears escaped my eyes as I lay there, reflecting on everything. This situation was far from what I had anticipated when I set off on this journey. I contemplated the events of the evening, the unexpected reunion, and the shared room that seemed to be an echo of our past. It was a night filled with nostalgia, uncertainty, and an undercurrent of something unspoken. The memories swirled in my mind like a bittersweet symphony, evoking emotions I had long buried.

One thing was certain, though – it was a night that had taken an unexpected turn, one that left me pondering the complexities of life, the resilience of human connection, and the mysteries of the heart. And as I closed my eyes, I couldn't help but wonder how the morning would be.

As I tried to sleep, my dreams were filled with fragments of the past: moments shared, promises made, and the heartaches that had defined our relationship.

The night seemed to stretch on, and as I slept, dreams and memories intertwined. My thoughts were a whirlwind of emotions, ranging from anger and hurt to nostalgia and curiosity. The past had resurfaced, and I found myself on an unexpected journey—confronting my fears, revisiting my history, and exploring the intricate blend of our relationship in the silence of the night.

As the sun began to rise, I freshened up and headed out to the beach. Rather, I ran away as I didn't want to be close to him and I was not sure what to talk to him. I had so many questions in those entire 10 years but now that he is in front of me, everything felt silly and meaning less. The sounds of the water splashing in the beach always calmed me. The place was peaceful and quiet. I continued to think about everything I wanted to say to him, all the questions I had in my mind, and what I truly desired.

Over the years, I realised that what I wanted most were answers to my questions. I had spent a long time trying to figure out what went wrong in our relationship, and in that process, I had stopped expecting love from him. I remember feeling heartbroken, losing a part of myself, and even trying to hurt myself. I was consumed by anger and pain, but strangely, I didn't feel the absence of his love anymore. It had faded away with time.

Then, as I stood there on the beach, I had a sudden realisation. Seeing him again did stir some old feelings, but it was also a moment of closure for me. I have to put an end to the constant thoughts that had tormented me for years. I have to let go of the pain I had sought, and I have to stop making him out to be the villain who had abandoned me. He was never responsible for me, and I couldn't force that on him.

It became clear to me that I was no longer searching for answers. It had been a decade, and his sudden appearance might have shaken me for a moment, but it would be unwise to let the past overshadow the present. Maybe he had followed me because he felt guilty or because he believed it was the right thing to do. I didn't want to know the reasons anymore. What I did know was that the chapter involving him is now closed. The things that had been causing me heartache had finally started to heal.

As I walked along the beach, the gentle touch of the water beneath my feet brought a sense of peace and contentment. The sun was beginning to rise, casting a warm and comforting light on the horizon. It was in this tranquil moment that I noticed a figure approaching in the distance – Varun. He appeared just as I remembered him, with a calm expression on his face. Yet, deep down, I knew that beneath that calm exterior, he, too, must have been feeling a bit unsettled.

As Varun drew nearer, he initiated a conversation, asking how I had been and attempting to explain himself.

"Don't you have any questions for me?" he asked.

"I did have lots. But I guess the answers don't matter now, do they?" I responded.

"Nice answer, babe," Gayatri said.

I chuckled. I can sense Gayatri raging inside, and if she were in Goa, she would have definitely given him a nice, tight slap at the least.

"Come on, continue," Shriya said, already biting through her nails. She can never handle suspense.

"Don't you want to know why I did that and what I have been doing all this time?" Varun asked me.

"I think I tried to find out enough, but you were not ready to share. I think it's a bit too late now to try to gather answers. I would just say I am glad you are doing well. I will only hope the best for you," I replied.

"I want to know about you, Disha. What have you been doing?" he persisted.

"You want to know how I survived without you?" I asked.

"Wow, what a bouncer," Gayatri said, sounding happy.

"Please don't be so caustic. I didn't mean it that way," Varun said.

"Awww, now I am feeling bad for him," Shriya commented.

Gayatri and Nisha looked as if she had gone nuts.

"Shall I continue?" I asked, smiling and enjoying all the emotions I am seeing in my friends. They just love me.

"Ya, ya, continue," Nisha said.

"You surely didn't want to be bothered by me in the last ten years. Why now? You didn't care what I was doing, whether I survived or not? Whether I killed myself. Nothing at all. So I guess me being caustic is obvious, isn't it?" I said very calmly to him.

"Babes…" Gayatri looked at me worriedly.

She has been there all the time, and she knows exactly what I felt when I uttered those sentences. I am sure she understood how difficult it was for me to say it out loud, to accept the fact that he made me vulnerable to the brink of being ready to hurt myself.

I nodded and continued.

"I don't have an answer for that. Now, if you put it like that, yes, you are right. I don't deserve it, or I don't have any right to ask you anything. I hope you will forgive me," Varun said.

"I did forgive you long ago. You don't have to worry. I don't hold any grudge against you. I am glad you happened to me; otherwise, I would never have come across lots of beautiful people in my life. I would have been stuck trying to make you happy. I am happy being myself. I am having the best life with the people who love and care for me. I will have to thank you for that. If you didn't leave me then, I would not have been in this place now," I said.

"What if I made the biggest mistake of my life, and I want to correct it? I want to set things straight. I feel like a fool now. I was selfish and arrogant. I felt I was more important. I didn't think anything about you or us," Varun said.

"What does he think of himself? Suddenly, he realises his mistake after seeing you by chance at the airport. Total bullshit, man. I hope you didn't melt to that, Disha," Gayatri said angrily.

Haha, Gayatri. You trained me well. That was exactly what I told him.

"Come on, Varun. You didn't even think about me until you saw me at the airport. Tell me honestly, if you didn't see me yesterday, we wouldn't have been having this conversation, and you would have been happy in your world and I in mine, right?" I said this to him.

"Good girl. What was his reply then?" Gayathri asked.

"Maybe it is destiny. That's why we met again after all these years. I am sorry; I know you are married and have a kid, but somehow, I am not able to give up on the thought that maybe we have a second chance," Varun said.

"What the hell. Destiny, my foot. When did you get married? What nonsense is he talking about? What second chance? This guy is so selfish, yaar," Nisha said before Gayatri could say anything.

"Lol, he heard me talk to Ananya, and he assumed that I am married," I replied.

"How stupid of him. He never realised how much you loved him, Dishu. Seriously yaar. He doesn't get it even now. How can he be such an idiot?" Gayathri said.

Shriya signalled to continue as Gayatri and Nisha went on ranting, and I continued.

"Firstly, I never married, and yes, I have a child. Her name is Ananya, though on records, she is adopted; she is totally mine. Destiny is decided by the choices we make. You always had a second chance all these years. You never wanted it. Now that you have seen me, you feel that maybe you did something wrong. Trust me, you have already made your choice, and I am sure you have been doing fine. As far as I am concerned, this is definitely a chance for proper closure. I am glad to know you are not dead and you have been successful in life. You got what you dreamt of, and I am sure you will only grow bigger. As for you, your guilt may be reduced. I don't know. Our relationship had an expiry date set by you, and it expired," I told him.

"You seemed to have distanced yourself. You sound very mature and not at all like the Disha I knew. I think maybe you are right. I did something that I felt was right back then. I thought you would move on and get married. I never, even in my wildest dreams, thought that you would become this amazing person I am talking to. I can feel the anger in you, but I guess that should be expected. I can't believe you adopted a kid. That tells me so much about you, and I didn't know this side of you. I was so wrong. I should not have done what I did," Varun said.

"Let's just say, maybe your moving away taught me a lot about myself, too. I had my good days and my bad days. I've had enough ifs and buts in all these ten years, but I moved forward. I am in a place where I am happy, and I think the same goes for you. I think this is it for us. I wish you all the very best with everything in your life," I told him with finality.

"Thank you, Disha. I know now I screwed up big time back then, but then, that is what I felt was right. I felt I was protecting you and me from the torment. I didn't know it would turn out like this," Varun said.

I listened intently as he continued to speak, his words carrying the weight of the past. "When I saw you at the airport, I couldn't help but feel that I had wronged you. It's not that I was unaware of it, but I made a decision that didn't leave room for you. Looking back, I realise it wasn't the wisest choice. I lacked the courage to end our relationship, and I knew you wouldn't have let me go easily. So, I convinced myself that I needed to stay away from you, and it was best for both. I threw myself into my work, never giving myself a moment to think. Perhaps if I had taken that moment to reflect, I might have made a different choice. I might have sacrificed my opportunities for the sake of our relationship, only to regret it for the rest of my life, and we might never have found true happiness. Maybe I should have tried reaching out to you sooner. I assumed you were married, and I didn't want to disturb you," he admitted.

"One thing I would say is, there would have been no need to sacrifice your opportunities or the relationship. You thought that was only way. You didn't think that I would have waited for you to achieve your dreams, and I would have achieved mine. I understand we were too young, but you decided on my behalf. Anyway, I agree with you, let's not disturb me now, and trust me, what you felt might have been correct. Maybe that was the best decision ever. We might have been a bad couple if we didn't choose different paths. No regrets at this point. Though it was completely your choice, your choice helped me understand what I didn't want in my life. I made choices that course corrected my life. I did lose precious years of my life, but I had to go through what I had to for no fault of mine. I truly came to believe that our choices make our destiny. ," I replied.

"You've had opportunities for a second chance throughout all these years," I continued, my voice steady but filled with emotions. "But you never seemed to want it. Now that you've seen me again, perhaps you're wondering if you made a mistake. Believe me, you made your choice long ago, and I'm sure you've been doing just fine. From my perspective, this is a chance for us to find proper closure. I'm genuinely glad to see that you're alive and successful. You've achieved your dreams, and I'm confident that you'll continue to accomplish even greater things. Maybe your guilt has lessened; I don't know. Our relationship had an expiration date, and you were the one who set it. That date has come and gone," I declared, bringing a sense of finality to my words.

"Wow, Disha. When did you become so mature," chided Gayatri, obviously happy with how everything went.

"Yeah, you gals trained me for years. I had to learn something isn't it? ," I said, smiling.

"What happened next?", Nisha asked. Well, Varun seemed taken aback by the boldness of my words. His voice carried a tone of surprise as he remarked, "You sound so different, more mature, and very adult."

I didn't say anything and smiled. I wished him good luck, and I left. Nisha replied.

"Wow, you are truly strong-minded, and he sounds rather narcissistic," said Nisha.

Her words reflected the stark contrast in character between the two of us. While I had found strength and closure in the encounter, Varun's words had unveiled a sense of self-centredness that had perhaps driven some of his past actions. It was a moment of candid reflection on the complexities of how relationships work and the different paths people take in life.

"Are you okay now? Are you really sure?" asked Gayathri. Her concern and worry were clearly evident in her voice.

With a hint of reassurance in my voice, I replied, "Yes babes, I'm planning to spend a couple more days here and take a proper vacation. Hopefully, I'll get fully charged up. Love you all a lot. I just had to share this with you. OK then, bye. We'll talk once I'm back."

As I ended the call, I couldn't help but feel grateful for the support and love of my friends. It was a reminder that even in the midst of life's uncertainties and unexpected encounters, the bonds of friendship remained a source of strength and comfort.

CHAPTER 2

DISHA IN GOA

"What a day," I murmured, feeling a surge of emotions that had lain dormant for so long. It was a strange relief to finally feel something again. Reconnecting with Varun after all these years had pulled back the curtain on a difficult truth: I had been living my life mechanically, sustained only by a fragile hope that my love wasn't just an illusion. My mind had been trapped in a web of "what ifs" and "maybes," each thought leading to more questions without answers.

For years, the sight of anyone who resembled him would make my heart skip a beat, a wave of longing and sorrow tightening in my throat. The last decade had been an emotional weight—like trying to keep my head above water in a vast sea of uncertainty. I'd been surviving, yes, but only just barely.

When I decided to talk to Varun this morning, I braced myself for the surge of emotions I had replayed countless times in my mind. I thought I would cry or perhaps lash out, cursing the years of hurt and questions that had haunted me. But instead, I found myself speechless, not quite ready to confront him initially, and instinctively wanting to escape. But then, I suddenly had a realizsation. He never reached out. He never tried. People often say that when someone you love leaves, the pain feels insurmountable, like life itself has lost meaning, leaving an irreplaceable void in its wake. But today, something felt different. I said goodbye to him—the only love I had known—and instead of despair, I felt a strange sense of relief, like I was finally beginning to heal, finally free from a burden I had carried far too long.

After seeing Varun in the morning, as I let those emotions run down my spine, I thought I would be crying or cursing as I imagined this scene in my mind over and over throughout the years, but I found myself at a loss for words. I found myself not ready to speak initially. I tried to escape. People often say that when the person you love leaves, it's a pain like no other. You feel as if life has lost its meaning, and an irreplaceable void gnaws at your heart. But today was different. I bid goodbye to him, my one and only love, but I feel the opposite. I feel like I started healing, like I am freed. I feel like a heavy weight has been lifted off me. I didn't seek answers from him that I have yearned for so long. I needed my closure. I needed it so badly that I waited years for it. I needed to know why he ghosted. Why did he leave me just like that? Why was I so unimportant to him? Why didn't my feelings matter to him? A constant thread of thoughts, meant to flow seamlessly, kept getting tangled.

Talking to Varun after all those years made me realise one thing. It is all in my head. I have been hoping to meet him someday, and I always wondered what I would say to him and how. Yet, when our paths finally crossed, everything became clear. I knew exactly what I wanted to say, and my intentions were as crystal clear as my thoughts. I simply understood he was not the right person for me. He didn't fit my puzzle. I was trying to force-fit him so that I could complete my picture. Fortunately, he is not the one to be part of my life. Yes, fortunately.

I spent the last decade in agony. I've spent countless days questioning what went wrong, where I faltered. My love for Varun ran deep, unwavering, and pure. I was willing to give up everything for him. I knew he loved me, too, but he loved himself more. It's absurd, isn't it? I didn't lose my love to someone else; I lost it to the very person I loved.

I was denied the opportunity to express my thoughts and feelings. But now, I am determined to reclaim my voice in my own life. I endured years of anguish and battled depression, merely existing rather than living. Ananya, my daughter, and my closest friends saved me from the depths of despair. There were moments when I contemplated giving up, fear and hopelessness gripping my soul. At the very least, I deserved a proper closure. Instead, I was ghosted—treated as if I never existed, as if I meant nothing.

Now, out of nowhere, he reappears after catching a glimpse of me as if he can simply waltz back into my life. It wasn't even a sincere attempt to return; it was a stroke of chance. If that chance of meeting hadn't happened, had that encounter not occurred, I doubt he would have spared me another thought for another decade.

I refuse to let him trample over me once more. I deserve better. I deserve to be cherished, valued, and truly treasured and loved.

I can't say that I'm experiencing happiness or sadness, or even if there's any pain. I think I feel a profound sense of tranquillity, serenity, and peace. This moment is just perfect. It marks the first time in a decade that I've been able to express exactly what I feel, to him and to myself. I had the opportunity to convey my emotions without resorting to tears, which always seem on the verge of escaping as if they hold a story of their own.

I knew I didn't want him anymore. I am at peace now. I feel like a heavy burden has decided to lift off my shoulders. The radiant sun and the harmonious waves meeting the shore create a sense of synchrony, as though a fresh day has commenced, filled with numerous treasures and the promise of a splendid day ahead.

I decided to go back to the beach in the evening. I feel there is so much to process. I sat in the room the whole afternoon and tried to flush out the thoughts.

Luckily, the beach is close by. I freshened up after my nap, quickly changed, and went to the beach. I approached the water, feeling the waves gently caressing my legs before receding, carrying the sand from beneath my feet. It's as though the waves are cleansing me, taking away whatever doesn't belong. I fixed my gaze on the waves, relishing the moment. The world seems to be getting better and brighter.

In that instant, a voice called out, "Hey, you in the yellow dress! Look out!" I swiftly turned around, only to be struck in the face by a volleyball, the impact nearly causing me to lose consciousness.

As I regained my senses, I was greeted by the sound of an amazingly sexy voice calling out to me. I opened my eyes to find myself gazing into a pair of the most enchanting brown eyes, filled with concern, belonging to a man who was incredibly close. I could sense the strength in his grip, and his scent emitted a delightful aura. He effortlessly carried me to a nearby seat, all the while repeatedly asking if I was alright.

I was utterly taken aback. I continued to gaze at him until he earnestly asked, "Are you okay?" His genuine concern was evident in every line of his face, making me want to reach out and assure him not to worry.

I was almost on the verge of touching his face when a group of guys suddenly rushed over, apologising profusely for the wayward ball. I quickly composed myself, muttered that it was right and hastily made my exit from the scene.

The intensity of the encounter was overwhelming. Each step back was a deliberate attempt to regain control, to shield myself from the vulnerability that had briefly washed over me. As I walked away, my emotions were a complex mix of apprehension, excitement, and a tinge of regret for letting my guard down.

With a rush of embarrassment, I realised how I must have appeared—disoriented and vulnerable. I could feel my heart beating so fast. I was scared and excited at the same time. I haven't been so close to a man in almost a decade. I had to shake myself out of it. I went back to the hotel, flustered and embarrassed.

I feel so stupid. I was almost about to touch his face. What on earth was I thinking? That guy was nice, though. His voice is so amazing and soothing. He looked genuinely concerned.

I could feel my heart pounding. I went blank for a moment when he was holding me. I checked my face to see if I got hurt. There is a slight bump on my head, but it should go away by morning.

It felt good, though. Maybe I should stay back in Goa and explore the place for a while. I am feeling all light and peaceful, like somehow all the weight I was carrying on my shoulders suddenly vanished, leaving me lighter and happier.

"All ok?" pinged Gayathri.

She still seemed to be concerned and worried. I am pretty sure she might be thinking so many things right now. She is no less of an overthinker than I am. Over the years, she became so protective of me. She is the best thing that happened to me in a time of need. It's interesting how some people come into your life when you need them most and how some go away when their time is done. Varun's time in my life was done, so he is gone forever. Gayatri came into my life, and she helped me find purpose in life with my little Ananya. I feel so blessed.

"Did something else happen? You are quiet," Nisha pinged too.

I guess they feel terribly disturbed due to the turn of events earlier today.

"All good, yaar. Planning to explore the place from tomorrow. I'm loving it here. Feels like a new beginning. Thanks a lot, girls. XOXO," I replied.

Shriya and Nisha dumped a load of emojis in the group chat.

I smiled at how they were competing with emojis.

I decided not to tell my friends about what happened after the beach encounter. I'll save that story for when we meet face-to-face. They will start getting more concerned and curious.

I feel like a new person. I don't want to remain the same old, worrying, risk-averse, and monotonous Disha. It's high time I started living my life and figuring out what I wanted from it.

My trip to Goa, started on a good note. What was bothering me for years suddenly got resolved, and I sense that more exciting adventures await if I embrace a carefree attitude. So, I freshened up and made up my mind to go out. It's the start of a new chapter in my life, and I'm eager to see where it leads me. I made a list of places to be visited most in Goa. I think it would have been great if the girls came over. It would have been an all-girls fun event, but it's not bad too. I had the biggest closure of my life, the one I never needed. I am feeling fresh, and I want to explore. This is definitely the new me.

"Let me see where this leads me to." Thinking that, I started out and decided to shop first as I didn't get a chance to pack right, for my dear girls did not let me know my destination. So I explored the Goan market; all the clothing was very vibrant and flowery, not at all my style, but who was there to question? I decided to explore all the weirdness and do the things that I don't normally do. Now is the time to let it all out. I bought some dresses and some wine. I went around to the beaches. Baga Beach was nice, bubbling with people.

Baga Beach is a perfect spot for adventure lovers, especially those who enjoy water sports. There's a wide variety of activities to choose from, offering excitement for every thrill-seeker. You can feel the adrenaline rush while riding banana boats and bumper boats or enjoy the fast-paced fun of water scooters and Jet Skis. For a calmer experience, dolphin cruises offer a peaceful way to see the beauty of the beach from the water. And if you're up for a real adventure, parasailing gives you a stunning view of the coastline from above.

I decided to try parasailing. It was an amazing experience. As I was lifted off the ground by the parachute, my heart raced with excitement. The feeling of being suspended in the air, with nothing but the vast expanse of sky above and the shimmering sea below, was absolutely exhilarating. With each gust of wind, I felt a rush of adrenaline course through my veins, propelling me higher and higher into the sky.

I looked down at the beach below. I couldn't help but feel a sense of wonder and awe. The world seemed to stretch out before me in all its glory, with the waves crashing against the shore and the sun casting a golden glow over the landscape. It was a sight unlike anything I had ever seen before, and I felt incredibly lucky to be experiencing it firsthand.

But amidst the excitement, there was also a profound sense of peace and tranquillity that washed over me. As I floated gently through the air, I felt free and one with the world around me. All my worries and cares seemed to melt away, replaced by a deep sense of calm and contentment.

It was a moment of pure bliss, a fleeting escape from the hustle and bustle of everyday life. As I slowly descended back to the ground below, I couldn't help but feel a sense of gratitude for the incredible experience I had just had. It was a memory that would stay with me forever, a reminder of the beauty and wonder that can be found in the simplest of moments.

I explored the place. It was full of tattoo parlours and tarot shops, spas, and some very legendary shacks. I kept on walking around, and I decided to get a tattoo. One of the things I never thought I would do, but yes, one more crazy thing added to my bucket.

෨ Fate Intertwined ෬

I walked into the tattoo studio, filled with a mix of excitement and nervousness. I had always wanted to get angel wings tattooed as a symbol of freedom, protection and spirituality.

The tattoo artist was friendly and reassuring, which helped ease my nerves. We discussed the design, and I chose a pair of angel wings with tiny details and soft, flowing feathers. As the artist began to work, I braced myself for the pain, but surprisingly, it wasn't as intense as I had imagined. Instead, there was a strange sense of comfort in the rhythmic buzzing of the tattoo machine.

The wings taking shape on my skin represented more than just a design; they symbolised hope, faith, and the belief that I am never alone, no matter how challenging life may become.

As the tattoo neared completion, I couldn't help but feel overwhelmed with emotion. Tears welled up in my eyes as I realised the significance of what I was doing. This tattoo was not just about aesthetics; it was a deeply personal expression of my innermost beliefs and values.

Leaving the studio, I felt a sense of peace wash over me. My angel wings tattoo will be a constant reminder that I am capable of overcoming any obstacle and that I am always surrounded by love and protection, both seen and unseen. It was a transformative experience that I will carry with me for the rest of my life.

CHAPTER 3

ARJUN

My phone kept buzzing incessantly, and I fumbled to find it with my eyes half-closed. It was Vivek, my friend, who was on the other end of the line, urgently trying to rouse me from my slumber.

"Arjun, wake up, dude! We need to catch the flight, man! Who sleeps at this hour?" he exclaimed, his voice filled with a mix of irritation and worry.

"Just a few more minutes, man. I've been working non-stop for 48 hours. Let me catch a wink," I mumbled in response, my words laced with the weariness of a sleep-deprived mind.

My dreamy thoughts continued.

I wanted to escape. I know it's not going to be an easy trip for me. For a moment, I thought I should get out of the plan before it's too late. I felt like a train of thoughts running through me.

Vivek pestered me a lot to get me to join the trip. He is my friend from the first day of college. We both were part of the same group of students who were ragged that year. It was fun, though. Vivek was made to run around the campus, and he was almost dehydrated. I was made to clean all the seniors' bikes. We shared a lot of fun acts after that day. The best thing was always the basketball game, which we played after hours.

We had a wonderful time in college, and then I went ahead to finish my Master's in the US. I was in the US all the while and came back to Mumbai after many years as I had some office work to complete.

"Everyone from college is planning to meet up at Goa," Vivek said.

"You know my answer," I replied.

"Yaar, come on," it's been ten years since we went to Goa. I think you should come this time. You have been away for so long. It will be good.

"Bro, you know the reason, don't you?" I said, not going into details.

"I know, that's why it is important for you to come. You should let go," Vivek said. I stuck myself to work and the hotel since I came back two weeks ago. I was planning to wrap up the work as soon as possible and go back to Boston.

Vivek wouldn't hear of it. "We are going for a holiday," he declared.

Arjun

"It's been ages since we met, and you are just going away? I am not taking any of this, man. You better stop running. Accept what has happened and start living. I am booking tickets for Goa, and you are coming. That's it," said Vivek.

"No, mate, I have to get back to work," I insisted.

"Then you can forget our friendship too," he responded angrily.

I sat down. I was about to retort with the response that would calm him, but then it's been long.

I should move on. I can't keep running away forever. I need to get over the memories. I need to be able to live, I told myself.

"Fine. I will try to come," I said, trying to stay non-committal.

"Hey, come on, we will miss the flight; wake up. You can catch that wink on the flight," yelled Vivek through the phone.

"Damn you, fine, I'm coming," I woke up lazily and dragged myself out. The prospect of missing our flight was not a pleasant one, especially with Vivek planning it all.

I hastily packed my essentials, summoning the last reserves of energy I could muster. Being a bachelor had its perks, one of which was the freedom to live life to the fullest. Weekends were the highlight of my existence, offering an escape from the monotony of the workweek. We partied like there was no tomorrow, and those moments were when my world truly came alive. However, weekdays were an entirely different story; I worked tirelessly as if there were no end to the tasks at hand. Still, I wouldn't have had it any other way. I revelled in the thrill of life's highs and lows. It keeps me busy, away from the memories.

As I made my way to the airport, I couldn't help but ponder the two sides of my world. The wind whipped through my car's open window, carrying with it the scent of rain, and the radio played a cacophony of inane songs. As I was about to change the station to escape the auditory assault, a new song began playing - "In dino dil mera..." Intrigued, I paused and let the melody wash over me. It was a pleasant tune, evoking nostalgia for the early 2000s when music seemed to possess a unique charm. Just as the song was about to conclude, Vivek called again, his voice filled with impatience, urging me to hurry.

I soon arrived at the airport, skillfully navigating through the labyrinth of parking lots. I parked my car and made my way to the departures area, where my group of friends was already assembled. The flight was scheduled to depart, but an unexpected two-hour delay lay ahead of us.

We decided to wander around. Some were on the phone, as expected, while some went ahead to the bar and lounge.

As I wandered through the terminal, my stomach began to grumble, reminding me that it's been a long time since I had a bite. Lost in thought, I inadvertently turned to find something to eat and collided with someone while making my way through the crowd. I turned around to find a lady and a gentleman stooping to collect their fallen belongings. Before I could offer assistance, my phone buzzed again, this time with Vivek's voice giving directions on where they were and that I should join them. With a hasty apology to the strangers, I sprinted to catch up with my friends. However, I couldn't resist stealing a quick glance back at the lady I had accidentally bumped into, only to see her hastily retreating from the scene with a bewildered expression as though she had just seen a ghost.

I shook my head, attributing her reaction to the everyday scenes of airport encounters, and rejoined my friends. With two hours to spare, we decided to pass the time by exploring every nook and corner of the airport's shopping area, much to the annoyance of the store attendants. The bustling atmosphere and constant announcements over the intercom added to the sense of excitement and anticipation.

Finally, after what felt like an eternity of waiting, the airline staff announced the long-awaited boarding call. We eagerly rushed to join the queue, determined not to get caught up in the inevitable chaos that typically accompanied the boarding process. Settling into my seat on the plane, I glanced around and saw her—the lady I bumped into earlier. There was an inexplicable serenity about her, yet an underlying restlessness seemed to simmer just beneath the surface. My curiosity began to stir once more.

I couldn't take my eyes off her as she settled into her seat. Unfortunately, my vantage point was far from ideal as I was seated several rows behind her. The seat beside her remained unoccupied, and a strange feeling gripped me – a faint hope that no one else would occupy it. A rather funny thought, I would say. I didn't want anyone else seated beside her. My thoughts were interrupted when a guy entered the plane and settled into the vacant seat beside her. There was a momentary exchange between them, their gazes locking in a way that hinted at familiarity. As the air hostess began her pre-flight announcements, I forced myself to shift my attention away from the intriguing pair and directed it towards the in-flight entertainment.

My mind wandered back to her. That fleeting encounter, so brief yet so impactful. There was something about her - a spark, a mysterious allure that I couldn't quite place. She was like a verse from an unfinished poem, leaving me yearning for more. I wish I could see her once again.

She is like a verse of an unfinished poem, a story yet to be told.

Her presence is the one in which you want to dwell.

Her eyes were deep with untold stories to keep.

Guarding the most prized possessions yet to seep

She is trying hard to be vulnerable.

She is scared of what might tumble.

ॐ Arjun ☙

Holding onto the thoughts together.

She embarked on her own forever.

She is not the one to ask.

She is not the one who suffers.

She shines with a light of her own.

Casting the warmth for you to surrender.

Never was it easy for her to trust.

Sometimes, it's easier to rust.

No wonder she is hiding her light.

for she is afraid of what the dark might

Trusting is never easy; it's simpler to conceal.

Sometimes, it's better to just let wounds heal.

She stands alone not because there is no one to hold

But she is the one who should be beheld.

As I wrote the sentences, a few tears found their way out, for I remember the last time I wrote something was for someone I loved. I tore the paper and hid my eyes with the cap. I didn't want to venture into that lane, for there was no coming back.

Vivek asked if I was okay.

"Yea, let me catch some sleep," I mumbled.

Vivek tapped my hand as if he knew what was going on in my mind.

I turned away and tried to sleep as the plane started to take off.

I was just closing my eyes, but the visuals kept pouring in.

The flashes of the girl in the front leaning over the window and closing her eyes, and those of the memories that I held too tight, the discussion I had with Vivek last Friday, kept running through my thoughts, and I tried to doze off.

CHAPTER 4

ASHA, MY FIRST LOVE

"*As soon as we reached Goa, Vivek had us running. We got to the resort, checked in, and the rest of the folks joined us. It was a college get-together. We were meeting after eight years, so lots of stories and beer. Everyone had a different story to tell. It's a good thing that Vivek decided to drag me here. I have been keeping myself so busy that I almost forgot some memories to hold. The guys went on pulling each other's legs, and the touchy topics of heartbreaks and first love started to pour in. I decided to sit this one out and started strolling along the beach. The calm of the waves hitting the beach, clear skies, and a beautiful moon. This is definitely what she would have loved. I remember the time when we both came to Goa. It was such a beautiful memory tucked away deep so that it wouldn't hurt me anymore.*"

As I walked along the sandy shore, the serene atmosphere, with waves gently lapping the shore, clear skies, and a beautiful moon overhead, was almost therapeutic.

Fate Intertwined

I found myself grateful that Vivek had persuaded me to come on this trip. My life had been a whirlwind of constant busyness, leaving little room for nostalgia or the recollection of cherished memories. But as we sat there, the gang engaged in friendly banter, I realised that some moments should be held onto despite the pace of life and the pursuit of success.

I couldn't help but reminisce about her. The tranquil beauty of the scene before me, so many of the moments we had once shared together in Goa, stirred my emotions. It had been a beautiful memory, one that seems to be nagging at me as while I keep trying to push away.

The night with my college buddies had been a blast, filled with drinks and endless conversations that seemed to transcend the passage of time. Eventually, as exhaustion caught up with us, we dozed off. As the first rays of dawn graced the horizon, we decided to kick off our day with a game of volleyball on the beach.

We woke up around midday after a lot of push and pull from Vivek. We went out to explore a bit of the market and gather some ingredients for the day ahead. We went out for lunch and enjoyed Goan delicacies. It's been ages since I have been carefree. After a little bit of exploring, we went back to our hotel and decided to go for volleyball on the nearby beach in the evening.

We started playing volleyball at the beach, with each one acting like a superstar and making a fool of themselves.

Asha, My First Love

Age definitely took its toll on some, leading to hilarious comments and rolling laughter.

We were having an absolute blast, the sand beneath our feet, the sun on our backs, and the salty sea breeze invigorating our spirits. Laughter filled the air as the game intensified. It was in the midst of this exhilarating play that an unforeseen incident occurred. The volleyball flew with unexpected force, sailing far beyond our intended target and heading directly for a girl who happened to be standing near the beach.

I immediately yelled a warning to her, but as she turned to respond to my shout, I began to slow down. To my astonishment, it was the same young lady I had encountered at the airport. Time seemed to stand still for a brief moment as I watched her in disbelief.

Before I could fully process the situation, the volleyball struck her squarely in the face. Ordinarily, such an occurrence might have elicited a chuckle from me, but this time, I was filled with concern. Instinctively, I rushed to her and caught her just as she was about to lose her balance and consciousness. Gently, I helped her to a nearby beach chair, holding her tightly and providing support to ensure she wouldn't fall.

At that moment, as I looked at her up close, I was struck by her vulnerability and innocence. Her features were delicate, her expression one of haziness and disorientation. She appeared so fragile, and a sudden urge to protect her welled up within me. It had been quite some time since I had experienced this instinctive need to safeguard someone. I was almost lost in my thoughts when the guys came running and started asking questions. She recovered quickly and rushed away from the beach. I was left at the place, thinking of Asha.

The guys went about playing the ball, but the brief encounter with the girl swept me away with the emotions I thought I had forgotten. I turned away from the group and stared out into the sea, and the memories flooded my thoughts.

Vivek's yelling brought me back to the present.

"The girl looked cute, right, bro?" he asked.

"Yes, she was," I said, looking back to where I sat and held the girl.

We went back to playing. I continued playing the ball, hitting it with such force that it reflected the turmoil inside me.

After some time, everyone gave up playing, started chatting, and lazing around. We went on about the day, explored the place, and it was a fun gathering with old friends.

Mornings are mostly not that happening, and most of them are still not over their hangover. So, I decided to go exploring alone. I rented a bike and went around the places in Goa. I kept driving in the small bylanes of Goa, exploring and unearthing the places I had never been to. I was almost about to hit a girl who abruptly came out of nowhere. She was wearing a very bright Goan dress, which was rather funny on her.

It's the same girl I saw when we were playing volleyball. She stared with such innocence that I forgot everything around me until she moved away, looking across. I saw that there were two dogs, and she seemed to be scared of them. I got off the bike, and she slowly moved behind me, away from the dogs, staring at them from my back. I don't know what it is about girls; the moment they are scared and reach out, they kind of make the man a hero. I chuckled with the thought in my head. I shooed the dogs away. She sweetly said thank you and moved as fast as she could in the other direction without even turning back. I think she was super scared that the dogs would follow her. It was a funny scene, though. I got on the bike and went off exploring the unknown. One thing in Goa, it's always good to ride bikes. It is easier to go through the small lanes, and you get to cover a lot.

By evening, I got a call from Vivek to reach the resort for the next adda, and I headed back. I went to my room to freshen up, and as I was taking my shower, I suddenly remembered that girl in the morning. It brought a smile to my face. She is beautiful in her own way, I thought.

Vivek kept buzzing my door. I came out of the shower and was like, "Let me have my bath, at least."

Vivek said, "What man, you are showering alone ! I was hoping to catch you red-handed with a girl."

"Just shut up," I said and dressed up to go.

We headed to our friends, and they started drinking already. As I settled in with my beer, listening to my friends reminiscing about the good old days, their words faded into the backdrop of my own thoughts. I slipped into the past I had tried to avoid remembering for years. Eight, to be exact. Life had taken an unexpected turn, and I tried to protect myself. I threw myself into work, immersing myself in the utter chaos of deadlines, meetings, and constant challenges. It was a deliberate choice to keep myself distracted and alive.

But in the quieter moments like this, surrounded by friends yet alone inside my head, the past slowly began to creep onto me. Her memories started to tug at me, taking me to the best days of my life. I remembered her beautiful eyes that always spoke multitudes, her laughter that used to fill my days, the shared dreams, and plans we made for the future. Those memories were like old photographs, faded at the edges yet vivid at the core.

I could feel the tears trying to escape my eyes. I decided to start moving. Taking a stroll along the beach, the cool breeze from the sea reminded me that the world is vast. With each step along the sandy shore, the grains of sand, cool and slightly damp beneath my feet, grounded me in the present yet echoed with the subtle sadness of nostalgia.

The patterns in the sky appeared to be like an endless canvas. The horizon, where the sea met the sky in a dark, blurry line, made me feel like both are holding on to their untold stories, trying to connect yet feeling far. Walking along the beach, the thoughts and the feelings began to surface. The tears that I had been holding back began to flow slowly and steadily as a silent, steady trickle, each drop a memory relived, an untold history.

It had been quite some time since I had let my thoughts wander back to Asha, especially to those carefree days when our paths first crossed.

It all began during our second year of engineering, a time when the college campus was abuzz with new faces and a palpable sense of excitement. Freshers roamed around nervously, uncertain of where to go, while the more seasoned students revelled in their newfound seniority, taking delight in the roles they now played.

Watching the interaction between the newcomers and the seniors during the ragging period was always entertaining. My friends, Vivek and Harsh, had taken it upon themselves to participate enthusiastically in this tradition. They devised all sorts of quirky tests and challenges for the freshers, making sure to get their fair share of laughter at their expense.

For instance, I remember one time when they asked a particularly unsuspecting fresher to count all the books in our college library. It was a colossal library, and the poor soul spent the entire day meticulously tallying each book, unaware of the prank being played on him. Another time, they assigned a task that involved a fresher jotting down the names of everyone entering the canteen and the items they ordered. The freshers earnestly complied, recording each meal and drink with utmost seriousness while attracting puzzled looks from the fellow students.

Some were handed silly challenges, such as carrying a balloon with them throughout the day, making for amusing sights as they went about their daily routines with these unusual companions. Surprisingly, many freshers took these playful tasks in stride, often even requesting more challenges to engage with their seniors in a light-hearted manner. On occasion, they were even asked to help us with our assignments, a task that made the workload seem a bit lighter during our college days of idling and enjoying the freedom that came with it.

College life had a way of surprising you when you least expected it. It was a time of new beginnings, budding friendships, and the thrill of discovering your own identity. For me, it was no different. My journey into the fascinating world of college began like a typical story, but little did I know that an unexpected encounter with a fellow student would set in motion a series of events that would change the course of my life.

It all started on a regular day at the bike stand. I had just parked my motorcycle and was preparing to head to class when I heard a polite voice behind me saying, "Excuse me, sir." Turning around, I found myself face-to-face with a young girl who appeared to be a fresher. Her bright, eager eyes sparkled with curiosity, and she held a pile of books in her arms. I looked at her with a puzzled expression, wondering what she wanted.

"Are you Arjun?" she inquired. "Can you please help me understand this problem?" She pointed to my notes.

"Where did you get these?" I asked, genuinely puzzled.

"Vivek sir gave them to me to complete his assignment, but I couldn't grasp how to solve this particular problem. Can you please assist me? I noticed your name on the sheet, so I thought I could ask you," she explained.

I was taken aback by her honesty and genuine approach. She could have simply copied the assignment and returned it, but instead, she sought to understand the material. Her actions piqued my interest.

"What's your name?" I inquired.

"Asha," she replied.

I simply smiled and stood my ground, patiently explaining the entire concept to her. She listened intently, asking questions along the way. Afterwards, she thanked me and departed.

As she walked away, I couldn't help but notice her petite stature and the tall heels she wore. Her ponytailed hair bounced with every step, and I found it rather cute.

Vivek came and slapped on my back stopping my lingering thoughts and we moved on to our favourite hangout place of Basketball court.

ॐ Fate Intertwined ॐ

The following day, while entering the canteen, I spotted Asha again, seated in a corner, engrossed in her work. She seemed so absorbed in her studies that she appeared unaware of her surroundings, completely focused. I couldn't help but think of her as a dedicated student, a bit of a nerd, perhaps.

There was something undeniably charming about her, a blend of innocence and self-awareness. I contemplated making my way over to her table but was promptly interrupted when Vivek pulled me over to join our friends. Ravi, Vivek, Rishi, and I had been friends since day one of college, enduring the ragging together and having our share of fun. We played various sports, but basketball was our favourite. Despite cricket being a national obsession, our college had an excellent basketball court, and it quickly became our favourite hangout spot.

Although I continued with my friends, my thoughts remained fixated on Asha. I wanted to speak with her, even though I wasn't sure what I wanted to say. There was something about her that kept drawing my attention to her. I kept catching glimpses of her every other day, either hurrying to class or chatting with her friends. My eyes perpetually searched for her. On days when I didn't see her, frustration would gnaw at me.

I felt an inexplicable urge to talk to her, but I couldn't pinpoint exactly what I wanted to discuss. It was the little things about her that intrigued me. Her fashion sense was unique, and she didn't conform to a single style. She seemed to explore a wide range of clothing styles, not adhering to the stereotypical "nerdy" appearance you might expect. She looked comfortable in her own skin. Sometimes, she tied her hair up, while other times, she experimented with different hairstyles.

Once, I couldn't help but stare at her when she had her hair down and a gust of wind tousled it around her shoulders. She appeared somewhat annoyed by the wind and swiftly tied her hair up. It was at that moment, with her glasses on and her hair neatly tied, that I found myself dangerously drawn to her. I felt my heart race and a strong desire to kiss her neck swept over me.

"Am I losing my mind?" I pondered. Luckily, I turned away to be caught up by my friends, and it took some time to settle my heart. It was a confusing mixture of emotions, and at the time, I didn't quite comprehend what was happening.

CHAPTER 5

OUR FIRST VALENTINE'S DAY

Valentine's Day is one of the best times to be at college. It's filled with lots of exciting moments. There are love proposals happening all over, and you get to witness some fun and crazy antics. Some people find new love, while others might experience heartbreak. You'll see couples running off together and many others blushing and enjoying the day. The atmosphere is entirely different from usual.

All day long, there are various activities happening across the college, even though they're unofficial. It feels like a day that can make or break many couples. Some leave the day with happiness, while others leave with broken hearts. Guys show off their bikes and strength, and girls dress up beautifully. Everyone is curious about who's with who, and there are even bets on which couples will last and celebrate Valentine's Day together the next year.

I parked my bike and went to our usual hangout spot. The place was vibrant and colourful. There seemed to be a mini-game going on, and my friends Ravi, Vivek, and Harsh were enjoying it. As I approached them, I noticed a group of girls blushing and running away as if they had seen something surprising. Behind them was Sameera, the college heartthrob, holding a bunch of roses and basking in all the attention. I just smiled at everyone who was captivated by her and continued toward my friends. But then, Sameera suddenly stepped in front of me, blocking my path. I looked at her questioningly, and she handed me all the roses she had and walked away. I could hear wows and boos from the crowd.

Ravi and Vivek bombarded me with questions about what was happening behind our backs. They were curious about Sameera and Arjun, and they wanted all the juicy details. I was just as confused as they were. I looked away and saw Asha staring at me with a slightly shocked expression. It unsettled me. I put the roses aside and locked eyes with her as she walked away towards the classrooms. I felt a strange urge to follow her; something felt different.

Amid all the chaos around me, my eyes were searching for one person—Asha. I couldn't get that look in her eyes out of my mind. I wanted to comfort her, to reassure her that everything was okay. But wait, what was she worried about? Why did I want to pacify her? Why was I even thinking about her?

ꙮ Our First Valentine's Day ꙮ

Damn, I like her. It hit me like a tonne of bricks. I didn't realise that I really liked her until today.

"I need to find her immediately," I thought.

I started searching all over the college, checking every place I had seen her before. I went to the library, the canteen, and even her classroom, but she was nowhere to be found. Rumours were spreading fast about Sameera making a move on me, but I couldn't care less. I was growing restless and anxious. I was about to check the computer science lab when Advait, a senior, and his friends confronted me. He was clearly angry about something and blocked my path. Frustrated, I pushed him away, and he punched me, saying that Sameera was his. He told me to stay away from her. I never saw that coming.

I thought to myself, "Fuck." I looked him straight in the eye and said that I needed to thank Sameera for helping me realise my love. I left him standing there, utterly confused.

Still, I couldn't find Asha anywhere. Was she hurt? Was she disappointed in me? My mind was filled with worry and confusion. I wanted to ask someone about her, but I didn't know much about her or her friends. I didn't want to jump to conclusions, either. What if she didn't feel the same way I did? I didn't even know what I was feeling, let alone what she wanted.

Vivek and Ravi eventually caught up with me and dragged me to a party. I was physically there, but my mind was somewhere else. People around me were celebrating life as if there was no tomorrow, but I was deeply disturbed. I excused myself and headed home, thinking about what to say to Asha or if I would even see her in college the next day.

Then it hit me. We had never spoken. Why was I so worried about what she was feeling? Why did I care so much about that hurt look on her face? I had this strong urge to see her, to explain things to her, to erase that hurt expression and to see her smile. It was a strange and powerful feeling I couldn't ignore.

I was restless the whole night. I decided to talk to her the next day at college. I went about again searching for her in all the places I saw her before, but I couldn't find her. Wherever I went, people assumed I was looking for Sameera. It was annoying at most. I didn't care much about it.

As I suspected, I didn't see Asha that day. I kept up my search. I was hesitant to ask about her to others, as rumours fly around a bit too much. My eyes kept wandering around the common classrooms, looking eagerly through the juniors as the groups of them kept going around.

I didn't listen to my classes that day. I hardly focused on anything. I couldn't score a basket on the court; my thoughts kept wandering. I didn't want to do anything at all. I just took my bike and drove off. I kept driving until my tank got empty. I reached the outskirts of the city and sat at the

༄ Our First Valentine's Day ༄

nearby Dhaba, staring at the sky. There was a lot of chatter around me, but I felt like I was lost somehow.

I spent the whole day riding through the places and finding new scenarios, exploring local food, and just driving aimlessly.

Chotu got me the food and lassi, and I realised my stomach was grumbling. I ate to my heart's full and kept driving until I got a call from mum. I then realised that it was too late. I spoke to her, promised to be back home in two hours, got the tank filled, and rode back.

As I was about to reach home, I skidded and fell down, bruising my knee and arms. Luckily, no major damage. I called Vivek and asked him to come over. He arrived and took me to the hospital. The bruises were quite deep on my leg, so the doctor gave me painkillers and advised me to stay back in the hospital to check for any concussions. I called my mum and informed her that I would be staying with Vivek for the night and asked her to get some rest.

The next morning, I woke up with my body aching all over. Vivek and Ravi were there, sheepishly looking at me, and mum staring at me furiously. I immediately forgot all my pain and started saying sorry to mum.

Mum, please don't be angry. I didn't want to bother you in the night. It's small bruises and no fractures too. She was very silent. Trust me, it's better to have your mum yelling at you than have her stay silent. I started showing my antics to my mum, till I heard a laugh from the door. I saw Asha there. I froze. She came with some other juniors.

I quickly sat up straight and realised the pain in my body all over, cringing a bit. I saw the look in her eyes change to worry. She came closer with a bouquet and a book and said, "Get well soon, Arjun, sir,"

My mum repeated, "Arjun, sir, are you guys ragging your juniors?" Mum asked angrily.

Aunty, no, we don't rag the juniors. You know it, right aunty. We are the good guys," Vivek feigned innocence.

Asha immediately said, "Aunty, no, we got used to calling all seniors as sir. It's a force of habit. Arjun helps us with understanding subjects when we have questions; we respect him a lot."

Listening to her calling my name felt nice. I wanted her to call my name again.

Her friends kept poking her as if to rush, so she just said, "Bye, sir. Get well soon." We will meet you at college and leave.

I asked mum to leave as she was getting late for the office. She insisted on staying back, but I shooed her away to avoid getting more scoldings. I told her Ravi and Vivek will stay with me. She warned them to be with me until she is back. They were more than happy to bunk college in my name.

ॐ Our First Valentine's Day ॐ

As soon as she left, the guys started off. We thought Sameera would be coming to you, but that's a new face. I told them that I was feeling tired and needed some rest and acted as if I was in pain. I simply wanted to close my eyes and reiterate what happened just now. Now, I really wanted to go back to college soon.

I was told I could go back home in the evening. Vivek and Ravi helped me get home safely. Mum wouldn't let me be. She started off with all sorts of fruits and veggies and healthy stuff. I couldn't say anything to her. I know I am her world, and anything related to me panics her. After dad passed away, she made me her centre of life, and she kept herself busy either with work or with me. I sometimes feel guilty for not spending enough time with her, but then she pushes me off to go and have fun.

As I lay down to sleep, mum asked, "Chinnu, who is that girl who came to the hospital today?" I got all alert. "She is my junior, mum," I answered.

"Only Junior?" she asked. I felt my face becoming red. "So far, yes, only junior," I said.

Mum and I are best friends. I share my true feelings with her. She knows me inside and out. I might look tough from the outside, but mum knows me too well.

She smiled and said, "I will wait to know more. Rest well now."

Mum made me rest for a couple more days. I was raring to go and see Asha once more. I wanted to talk to her. I didn't know what I would say, but I just had to see her.

I struggled a lot to stay at home and recover for a couple of days. Without being sure of why I want to see Asha, I can't even ask my friends to find out about her. They will make a huge scene out of nothing. I kept waiting patiently to get back to college so that I can meet Asha and ask her.

As soon as I was able to walk, I went to college very early. I know one thing: nerds tend to be early to college and they tend to avoid unnecessary delays. I felt that Asha was one of the people who preferred to be early rather than late.

I started searching for her in the classrooms, then the canteen, and I couldn't find her. I searched for her in all the places where I had seen her before, but I couldn't find her. Then I remembered the library.

I rushed to go to the library and searched for her. There I saw her finally, stuck with a pile of books. She had her hair tied up and was wearing a white top and jeans. A perfect, cute button of a nerd. I went to her with my leg still bothering me; I was stumbling a bit. She looked up and just stared at me out of concern.

I could feel my heart melting away with that look of hers.

"How are you feeling now, sir?" she asked.

Oh God, this girl is killing me with cuteness, I thought.

ॐ Our First Valentine's Day ॐ

"I am better," I said, finding my words.

"That is great to know," she said.

I stood there with a what-should-I-say-next kind of situation, and she kept staring at me.

I was at a loss for words, wondering what to say next.

She simply stood up and said, "Let me take these books and come out to talk to you."

I felt relieved.

I stepped out and waited for her. It felt like an eternity to wait for her outside the library.

Soon, she came out, walking cautiously over the steps that threatened to make you take a fall. Generally, in the movies, this is where the girl slips, and the guy miraculously catches her over slow-motion music, with books flying everywhere, and their eyes meet, and voila, the audience knows that they fell in love with each other. But then this is no movie, and we were no actors, and nothing so romantic happened.

She came out and walked ahead of me, leading the way, and we sat in a nice, sweet spot where we were to ourselves.

I cringed a bit as I sat.

She noticed and asked, "Is it hurting?"

"Yes, a bit," I said.

"How do you find college?" I asked, trying to initiate the discussion after a bit of silence.

"Is that what you wanted to ask me?" she said with a very straight face.

I fumbled and mumbled. It was a total bouncer for me. I wanted to ask her a lot of things, but I didn't even know what to say. I had to practice a lot in front of the mirror to be able to even open my mouth in front of her, and her direct questions made me feel silly.

"No," I said.

She looked at me as if taunting me to put through the questions in my head. I then decided to cut the chase and be straightforward.

With my heart pounding like a drum, I took a deep breath and finally mustered the courage to confess what had been building up inside me for so long.

"I have been wanting to tell you something," I began.

"I can't hold it any longer. I feel restless. The very first time I saw you, you came to me to ask about the assignment, and I was curious about you. I didn't think much then, and we hardly ever spoke. But on Valentine's Day, when I saw you going away, I had a weird feeling as if you were going away from me. I felt like I upset you somehow. I couldn't figure it out then, but soon I realised that I am attracted to you. I don't think I can name a relationship at this point, but I want to tell you that I want to know you better. I hope that is okay with you." I said it out and held my breath, awaiting her response, hoping that she wouldn't laugh at me or stomp all over me and walk away.

She took a pause and seemed to be thinking.

She looked towards me and said, "Thank you for being straightforward. I totally appreciate you being honest about what you are feeling. Not many can express it clearly. I was wondering what you would call this feeling. I agree with you. I feel a kind of pull towards you. It could be because of the respect I have for you as my senior and as someone who is not bothering the freshers, and maybe because of what I heard about you. I kind of feel that attraction, too. I have not been able to understand what it is, but I do want to explore the feeling. I felt so worried when I learnt about your accident. I came rushing to see you. I did not speak much to you before, but that one moment, I felt like I needed to see you."

That was the beginning of our journey.

CHAPTER 6

FINDING OUR PASSIONS

The next few days were amazing. Asha and I met often; we spoke a lot, and much of it was more of discussions and learning in the initial phases. We explored our dreams, passions, the values we believe in, and what we like the most and hate the most. Many times, we were finishing each other's sentences. It was beautiful finding someone who is able to comprehend what your thoughts are. We never missed our college but had our share of fun. We had secret codes; we met at the café in one of the unfrequented places by our classmates, and we went on long drives.

Ravi, Vivek, and Harsh soon found out about us, and their teasing knew no bounds. Our gang soon grew with Asha's friends Meera and Rahini joining us.

Oh, the joys and woes of engineering life! We battled exams, pulled all-nighters, and argued passionately about everything from programming languages to the best places to find late-night chai. Our professors never knew whether to be impressed by our technical prowess or amused by our antics.

We all had our dreams and goals charted out. Asha and I wanted to go do our Masters, and we applied to the same colleges. I planned to work for a year before heading for an MS so that Asha and I can go together. Ravi had plans to take over his family business. Vivek got into the tech world through campus placements, and Harsh decided to become a pilot after four years of engineering. We tease him to no end.

We all wanted to make our friendship more memorable. So we made a plan to drive to Goa because why do something so routine as flying? We thought we needed to make this the best memory ever, and what's better than enjoying the scenic route of the Konkan coast with beach stops all the way and all of us on bikes? We planned the trip for months. There were so many things to consider, and we worked out the routes, which road to take, where to halt, and where to stay. Our plan was simple: to stick to the coastline as much as possible to enjoy the beauty of nature.

Asha was crazy about bikes. She always jumped at the thought of going for a ride. She enjoyed simple things in life. Of all, her love for chai is the most annoying one. She would randomly want to have tea at any tea stall. I wanted to take her to posh restaurants and all, but she was always happy with the cutting chai.

Finally, the D-Day arrived.

"Let's make this journey unforgettable," shouted Vivek over the roar of the engines, and we all set off. It was the most beautiful journey. With Asha hugging me close and the slight drizzles on the way, the beauty of nature surrounding us and the music roaring in our ears, it was the most beautiful feeling ever.

Asha and I lagged the group at times, lost in our own world. There was a comfort in our silence, the kind you only find with someone who understands you without words. With her arms around me, teasing me with silent signs, I felt like I was floating into a dreamland. Our bodies hugged each other, and she hugged me tighter whenever there was a curve. It made me go slow and enjoy the moment. The rush we were feeling within us and the lush greenery of the Western Ghats around us, so deep and vibrant, it almost seemed surreal.

"Beautiful, isn't it?" Asha said, her voice a soft melody against the backdrop of the Ghats.

"Like a dream," I replied, knowing I wasn't just talking about the scenery.

The beauty of the Western Ghats is a sight to behold.

"Let's stop here for a bit," I suggested, pulling over at a viewpoint. The group agreed, eager to stretch their legs. We stood there, looking out at the cascading waterfalls and the valleys shrouded in mist. It felt like we were on the edge of the world.

Asha stood close, her hand finding mine. Our fingers intertwined naturally, a silent acknowledgement of the bond we shared. I wanted to tell her so many things, but the words seemed unnecessary, lost in the beauty around us. The mist was around us, and it started drizzling a bit, making others run for shelter in the nearby café. However, when Asha looked into my eyes, I couldn't move an inch. I drew her closer into my embrace and leaned closer to her. She tipped her head in anticipation, lifted herself up with her body close to mine, and we kissed, slowly and passionately exploring each other. It was irresistible. It was hard to break off, but Asha gently tugged my shirt, suggesting we move to the group. I let her go reluctantly.

We held each other's hands and walked slowly towards the group. Everyone was busy getting some chai, and of course, Asha's eyes lit up at the chai, and we joined others in the discussion. My fingers made love signs in her palm, and she kept blushing and trying not to giggle. We were having our moments among everyone. While the chatter continued out loud, our inner turmoil and the desperate need to be close to each other continued, too.

The scent of freshly cooked parathas and the sizzle of spices filled the air as we feasted on. Full and satisfied, we continued our journey, stopping occasionally at scenic viewpoints to capture the breathtaking landscapes of the Western Ghats.

And when we finally arrived in Goa, weary but elated, it felt like we had conquered the world. As we dismounted our bikes and looked out at the shimmering sea, I couldn't help but feel grateful for the journey we had shared – a journey filled with laughter, love, and unforgettable memories.

For the next day, everyone had their own plans. We already had an exhausting ride, so many decided to sleep in. Asha would never. She had the day planned. We decided to go to Netravali Falls, a journey from the coast into the heart of Goa's lush countryside. Everyone had a hearty dinner and dozed off.

I woke up to the gentle sounds of the waves crashing against the shore at the beach, the early morning sunlight casting a warm glow on the sands. As I was lazily stretching, my phone pinged.

"Good morning, sweetheart. Are you up? Will you be able to drive, or do you want to rest?" said the message from Asha.

I chuckled at her message. It had so many hints that she would really want to go, but she understands if I am not up for it. I am able to decipher her messages now, I thought.

"I am not going to miss this chance of being alone with Asha," I thought to myself and responded, "Will be ready in 30 mins. Is that good for you, or do you need more time?"

Knowing her, she is already ready and waiting for me to sleep enough, according to her, and gently wake me up if I didn't already.

"I am ready already, will wait for you to freshen up," she said.

I smiled, realising I was right. This is going to be a beautiful day, I thought.

I quickly got ready, and, with a sense of anticipation, I checked over my bike, ensuring everything was in place for the long ride ahead. As I donned my helmet and sunglasses, I couldn't help but feel a thrill at the adventure that lay before me.

The morning air, cool and briny, filled our lungs as we prepared our bike for the journey ahead. "Ready for an adventure?" I asked. Asha responded with an excited nod, her eyes sparkling with anticipation.

The streets of Calangute were quiet in the early morning, with only a few early risers and local vendors beginning their day. I navigated my bike through the awakening town, feeling the cool breeze against my skin. The road ahead promised an escape into the serene beauty of Goa, far removed from the usual tourist locations.

We rode through, stealing glances and sharing smiles, the bike humming beneath us. Leaving the familiar behind, we ventured into the verdant embrace of Goa, with Asha pointing out every sight she found cute and odd along the way, her laughter a melody against the backdrop of our journey.

As we travelled further, the landscape transformed, offering us glimpses of Goa's hidden beauty. We passed through villages where time seemed to slow, sharing waves with the locals whose lives painted a picture of serene simplicity.

Finding Our Passions

"Imagine living here," Asha whispered, her head resting on my shoulder as we rode. I could only nod, caught up in the peacefulness that enveloped us.

Approaching Netravali National Park, the air grew cooler, the forest denser. We made an entry and paid the fees. We parked our bikes and, hand in hand, approached the falls. Netravali Falls is truly a hidden treasure within the Netravali Wildlife Sanctuary. The path to the waterfall is an adventurous one, with thrilling trails and lush forests, ultimately leading to a tranquil lake. We held our hands and trekked slowly through the area, enjoying every small moment. The distant sound of the falls called to us a natural siren song that felt peaceful. And then, breaking through the canopy, we were met with the sight of Falls - simply serene, a testament to nature's beauty.

The mist kissed our faces, the roar of the water enveloping us in its might. Asha's eyes mirrored the wonder I felt, her hand tightening around mine. We stood in silence, letting the beauty of the moment sink in.

Finding a secluded spot, we shared whispers and dreams, and the falls were witnesses to our promises and hopes. Asha sketched the scene in her journal, her fingers capturing the magic before us. I watched her, thinking how lucky I was to be sharing this moment, this life, with her.

At that moment, when Asha was going about her sketch, I kissed her cheek lightly. Her immediate reaction was to check the surroundings.

I got cheeky and said, "So, is it okay to kiss now when no one is around?"

Asha blushed and pushed me away. We were sitting on a small rock, and I tumbled over into the water as I slipped. Asha burst out laughing. I came out and dragged her as well into the water and teased her. I remembered the very old Liril ad of Preity Zinta and enacted it in the water. Asha couldn't control her laughter due to my stunts. I moved closer to her and pulled her toward me.

She pushed me away and swam toward the falls. We spent some time there and then came out. The ride back was quiet, with a comfortable silence between us as we processed the beauty we'd witnessed. Asha leaned against me, her presence a warm comfort as the scenery blurred past. We stopped once at a roadside café, sharing a meal and laughing. Our conversation was light and filled with the joy of our shared adventure.

As Calangute came into view, the setting sun painted the sky in hues of gold and orange, a perfect end to our day. We returned to the beach where we started, the sand cool under our feet as we watched the day fade into the night.

"Our little adventure," Asha said, her head resting on my shoulder. I wrapped my arm around her, feeling an overwhelming sense of love. This journey, to the serene wilderness of Netravali, was more than just a day trip. It was a chapter in the story of us, filled with sweet nothings and

Finding Our Passions

whispered dreams, a day that would remain etched in our hearts forever.

We reached our resort and met up with the rest of the gang. Each one shared the stories of their day, and Asha's excited, animated smile was enough to know that she is happy. I kept watching her and listening to her version of the day. It was just a beautiful moment that stayed with me forever.

While I was lost in my thoughts, Vivek came from behind and slapped my back, bringing me back to the present.

"Where are you lost?" he asked,

"Our bike ride," I responded.

"Hmm, good old days," he said and sat down calmly, watching the waves with me and drinking beer.

After some time, one of the guys called, and Vivek left, leaving me with my thoughts.

I sat there in the sand, watching the water touch the shore and go back, just like my grief tugging my heart and going back.

CHAPTER 7

THAT FATEFUL DAY

As the end of our four-year adventure approached, I decided to pop the question to Asha before we left for MS. All of us concocted a plan involving hidden treasure maps, bizarre clues, and a proposal at Mumbai's famous Marine Drive. Having so many friends is an added advantage.

I called Vivek and told him the plan. I decided to make her pre-birthday a big event and lay out treasures of gifts for her all over the place before midnight, and I wanted to propose to her on her special day. I really hoped she wouldn't get pissed off as I made her go all over the place. She always loved solving puzzles.

Everyone got super excited, and we went about executing the plan. I made sure that her best friend, Rahini, was with her so that I could know what Asha was doing and where she was going.

I sent Asha the message, "Meet me at the first place we met."

Asha looked at the message and is thinking about where it was. Rahini messaged promptly, giving me a scene-by-scene view of what is happening.

"Arjun is asking me to meet at the first place we met. I think it was the library. Let us go there; looks like he has something to say," Asha said excitedly to Rahini.

Rahini had big trouble acting curious and following Asha.

Asha reached the library and looked at the place where they spoke their mind out for the first time. She realised that is not the place to be. Then she remembered Valentine's Day and thought he meant the basketball court. She ran over there, but there was no sign of Arjun.

"Where is he?" she wondered.

"Oh dear, she is making me run all over college," lamented Rahini over the group chat we created for this purpose.

I chuckled.

Asha kept thinking where it could have been. She thought, could it be the hospital? Naa, that was not the first time.

Then she suddenly remembered, of course, near the bike parking.

As soon as Asha reached the bike park, she got a message.

"Hmm, that took you a while, dumbo," Arjun pinged.

"Now look for your favourite thing. There is a clue inside," said another message.

That Fateful Day

She gleamed. Of course, it was Arjun's bike, and he looked for a clue inside it.

The clue said, "Where the sea greets our city's history, find the arch that has witnessed many a story. Find the person with a blue balloon there to find the next clue."

Harsh was there near the Gateway of India, holding a blue balloon. Poor thing, he had to wait too long. Logical clues were easier for my darling, so she wasted no time reaching there.

Harsh gave her a big smile and handed her the next clue, along with a box of chocolates.

It said, "Seek the palace where kings dine; find the Middle Eastern flavours of the Arabian line. Find the table reserved for you and enjoy the meal as you do."

Asha looked at the clue and smiled. Rahini was still tagging along. I had to make sure that they were well-fed, too; otherwise, they would kill me. So, a small treat for my loved one.

"Looks like Arjun decided to tease me today," Asha said happily to Rahini.

"Well, sounds like fun to me. So, tell me, where are we headed?" Rahini asked.

"It's the Taj Mahal Palace, of course," Asha said.

As she entered, she was taken to her table, and all the food she loved was pre-ordered. I didn't want to waste too much time as she takes a hell of a lot of time to figure out what to eat.

"Arjun knows me too well," Asha thought, and Rahini echoed the same.

Both had finished their lunch, and the waiter came to her with the bill.

Asha looked a bit worried as she didn't pack for the huge bill. She worriedly opened the bill, only to find the next clue. She sighed with relief.

The waiter smiled and said, "The bill is paid for, and all the best for the next clue."

The clue said, "Near the sea, an old parlour stands, serving ice cream sandwiches in your hands. Now that you had a good meal, how about an ice cream?"

The waiter paused for her to read the clue and then gave her the next gift wrapped in gold foil.

She opened it up to find her favourite-coloured dress.

Asha immediately said, I know the place.

We frequented that spot so many times, so she would know that easily.

Rahini and Asha started to enjoy the ride, much to my relief. They reached the place and had a hearty ice cream.

I had Ravi waiting for them there. Once they finished their ice cream, he went to them and gave the next clue and her next gift.

That Fateful Day

She opened the gift to find an assortment of books she wanted. She loves tiny stuff.

Asha was not a spoilsport, and she didn't ask or call me. She followed the lead and decided to go ahead with what I had planned. She immediately got excited at the next clue.

"I am loving this," she said to Rahini and Ravi.

The clue said, "On an isle joined by a narrow path, a shrine that stands the sea's wrath. Find the man with an orange-coloured shirt holding onto a green balloon to find the next."

Asha wondered what that place could be for a while.

"Where to next?" Rahini asked.

Asha showed her the clue.

"Shrine is a place of worship, isn't it?" quizzed Rahini.

"Yes, you are right. It might be Haji Ali, isn't it?" asked Asha.

"It could be," replied Rahini.

"Let's go," Rahini prompted as she started to get desperate to meet the end.

They rushed to the Haji Ali dargah. The evening started to become more beautiful. They reached the middle of the path to find Vivek holding a green balloon sheepishly.

He wore the most colourful shirt he could wear. Poor thing, he was looking like a clown.

I love my friends; they did so much for us and our love.

Asha ran to Vivek, and he gave her the next clue.

"How many more?" she asked him.

"This is the last," Vivek smiled and replied.

"Oh," she said, sounding disappointed. She sometimes forgets that the puzzles need to end. Silly one.

He also gave her the next gift. It was the bag, exactly the one she loved to have.

She smiled. Then, they all decided to come together to the next stop.

"At the city's edge where land meets the sea, find the necklace that sparkles free," the clue said.

That was the last stop for us. She was to come to our favourite spot at Marine Drive. They all took the cab and reached Marine Drive.

She called me up, super excited about everything. "I love you, Arjun," she yelled, unable to contain her excitement. I could hear her happiness over the call.

I was waiting eagerly near Marine Drive with a bouquet of red roses and another full of colours. I had a bunch of balloons tied up nearby for her to be able to find me. I was super excited, too. Loving her has been a great part of my life. As we were venturing into the next phase of life, I wanted to proclaim my love for her and ask her to marry

That Fateful Day

me. I spoke to her parents already. They had a hint of what was going on. Her dad was initially hesitant as we were too young for marriage. I shared our plans for the future, and I assured him that once we finish our MS and settle into our jobs, then we will plan for marriage. He seemed impressed with the way we were planning, and he gave us the nod. Uncle and Aunt had plans for her birthday as this was her birthday just before we left for MS. So, I planned for a pre-birthday surprise followed by dinner with the family. Mum knew all the details about our love, and she, too, was to join the post-surprise dinner. We had it all planned to the dot.

I kept waiting eagerly for her. As the cab reached the place, Asha sprinted to me, jumped onto me, and hugged me tight. She showered me with kisses without caring about others.

I had to stop and control my laughter. She was clearly happy and acting like a kid. I tried to hold her on and asked, "Ma'am, can I propose to you now?" as innocent as I can be.

"She responded with a no, shaking her head from side to side."

I was taken aback. I got confused by her response.

She smiled, went down on her knee, and proposed to me.

"Mr Arjun, would you like to marry me? Do you think you can handle my tantrums throughout your life? Will you be my partner in crime and my travel partner for the next 60 years? Will you say yes to anything I ask?" she went on.

I kept laughing. I pulled her up close. I said, "Yes, madam, as you say. I will also take care of you. I will make love to you every single day. I will shower you with kisses, and I will change the nappies of our kids, too. We will be good partners. We will have our fights, and we will make out, too. We will travel the world and build our beautiful home, too. We will have our own share of troubles. We might fight. We won't be equals, but we will fill our home with our 100% together."

She blushed at my response.

"So, shall we marry?" I asked.

"Now?" she asked innocently.

"Not now, silly, after we finish our MS and find Jobs," I replied.

"So long? I can't wait to be with you," she said.

"So much drama," I laughed.

Her phone started ringing.

She picked it up; it was her dad.

She panicked a bit as it was too late and said, "Papa, sorry, I will start for home now."

"Turn to your left and see the other side of the road," her dad said.

ಌ That Fateful Day ଔ

He was with his aunt and mum, holding balloons, and they waved at us.

She looked at me in disbelief. She was a tiny bit worried about whether her parents would agree to our relationship, but looking at them all, she understood everything was sorted.

She was in tears. She hugged me tightly and said, "This is the happiest day of all."

She immediately turned and started to run towards her parents while I was picking up her presents and thanking my friends for spending the entire day helping out with the proposal.

But life has a way of throwing curveballs when you least expect them. Just as she was crossing the road to reach our parents, she didn't see the car coming in at speed, and it hit her. She flew in the air and was hit by another car coming through the other end, and she got run over by a bus.

She left me just like that. For no fault of hers. For being with me, for loving me.

I ran to her, I held her and cried.

I didn't understand what was happening. Vivek called an ambulance. People gathered around us. I kept calling out to Asha. She lay in my arms, lifeless, clutching onto the last clue to meet me near Marine Drive at the place we always sat.

She was wearing my favourite dress, now covered all with blood.

Tears kept rolling off my face uncontrollably, and I kept staring at the sea, reliving every moment of that day. Being back is painful, and I avoided it for so long, but this time, I thought I might be able to handle it. I couldn't. How can I when every little thing reminds me of her?

I let the tears flow, each one a testament to the love we shared, to the pain of losing her. They're a part of this journey, a journey of grief and healing that I'm only just beginning to navigate. I talk to her, telling her about my day, about the little things that remind me of her. The pain of speaking into the silence is sharp, but it's a pain I welcome. It makes me feel closer to her, if only for a moment.

The night grows deeper, and the chill of the evening air wraps around me. I should head back, but I'm not ready to leave this place, not yet. I pull my jacket tighter around me, a feeble barrier against the cold. It's funny, the things we hold onto. This jacket was a gift from her, a random present on an ordinary day. I loved it because it came from her, but now, it feels like a piece of her, something I can cling to in her absence.

As my tears subsided, I kept looking at the sea. The waves gently touched my feet as if telling me it was okay. I feel like the vibe around me is trying to tell me something. The night is pleasant as if everything is normal. I felt like I was not alone; she was looking at me, maybe sad, maybe with a smile. My heart ached at the thought. I love her deeply, but I began to think, what if I am not letting her go? What if she is waiting for me to come to terms with it? What if she is just there beside me, wishing for me to heal?

The logical mind began to act. It is okay to feel the pain. I need to live on. I need to live for myself and mum. I haven't been myself for ages. Mum stood by me silently, understanding my pain. She knows the pain of losing someone. She lost dad at an early age, and she lived on for me. She never spoke about her pain. I don't remember seeing her cry. She is so strong. A sudden realisation hit me. Mum has made me her world and has lived on through the pain without letting me realise what she has gone through.

I have been so stupid and selfish. I have been thinking of Asha the whole time, despising myself for what happened and never realised how mum has been constantly and silently bearing my pain and trying her best to be with me. I am sure she might have relived all her pain during this time, and I didn't bother to reach out to her. I was so offhanded and so full of myself that I forgot all about mum,

That realisation hit me like a tonne of bricks. I called mum immediately. She picked up.

"Arjun, why are you calling at this time? Are you okay? What happened?"

"Maaa...," I said, with tears rolling out again.

"Were you thinking about Asha?" she asked immediately.

"Yes," I replied.

She immediately said, "Arjun, she was a nice girl, but you should let her go. You can do nothing to stop the fate. Life is like that. Sometimes, there are no reasons why things happen when they do. It is a constant reaffirmation that there is some superpower that exists, balancing what we need to do. You need to forgive yourself. It is not fair to you. Fate acts that way. Sometimes, there are situations that happen for a specific reason, and we humans cannot understand that. You need to move on. Life is still beautiful; some memories are tough to deal with, but you need to let go of the past. You cannot change it. Accept it and live your life."

"How can I let her go, mom? It feels wrong. I feel wrong to give up on her. I feel like I am cheating if I forget her," and I started crying.

Mum, on the other side, let me cry till I started sniffing up.

"Where are you?" she asked.

"Mum, don't get angry. I am in India. I came to Goa. I am sorry, maa. I am sitting here and crying about my girlfriend, but I never realised or thought about the pain you might have gone through when you lost dad. I don't think I can ever forgive myself for being so stupid. Maa, I am sorry for not caring enough for you," I tried to continue and started crying all over.

"Enough of your crying now. I am glad you are in India, and you must be proud of yourself for making it here. I know you are there. Do you think I will let Vivek be without knowing your whereabouts? Anyway, I know what you might be feeling; let them all come out. Enjoy your stay in Goa as much as you need, and if possible, come and meet me before you go," mum said.

"Mum don't say it like that. Now I feel even worse. I will take the next flight and come to you. I miss you a lot, mum. Sorry for shutting you out, too. I was too full of myself. It just hit me now that I was acting up. I will come right away," I said, determined to meet her.

"Too much drama, shut up and enjoy the vacation. Be there as long as you like. We will have plenty of time to talk later. Enjoy and feel refreshed. Come home when you get to; I am not going to wait for you. You just come whenever you feel like," mum said, smiling.

"Thank you, mum. I love you lots. You know that, right? You are the bestest mum in the whole world," I said.

"Ufff... how many times should I tell you? There is no such word," mum said, feigning annoyance.

"There is, in my world. You are the bestest mum ever. Now go to sleep. Sorry, I woke you up. I will let you know when I land in Mumbai," I said.

She said goodbye and ended the call.

I feel a sense of peace, a quiet assurance that I'm not alone. Mum has always been with me. Asha is also with me, in the stars, in the sea, in the very essence of who I am. And with that knowledge, I find the courage to face another day, to embrace life with all its pain and beauty. For her, for me, for the love that will always bind us, I will keep moving forward, one step at a time.

I started to think about the future, a future without her, and it felt like standing on the edge of an abyss. The path ahead is unclear, shrouded in fog, and I'm terrified of taking the next step. But I know I must. Neither mum nor Asha would want me to stay lost in this grief forever. Finding the strength to move forward and live a life that honours Asha's memory is perhaps the hardest challenge I've faced and will face. But it's one I must accept, for her and for me.

The waves touched my legs gently, caressing as if trying to say it was okay.

"Do you mind me joining you?" someone said.

I turned towards the voice and saw the girl from this morning. At that moment, a tear was about to escape my already red eyes. I turned away to clear it and said, "Yes if you would like to get bored. I am not a great company at the moment."

She smiled and said, "That is ok. I am a bit scared of the dogs around here, but I want to look at the sea. So, if you don't mind, I want to sit a bit closer to you so that I don't freak out."

"I swear I won't bother or pull you out of your solitude," she said with such an innocent face.

ஸ That Fateful Day ௸

I burst out laughing, which turned into a cough, and I motioned her to sit beside me.

"I'm Disha, by the way," she said, fishing out the water bottle from her bag.

Arjun, I replied.

She sat silently, and I continued to stare into the sea.

"How is your head, by the way?" Arjun asked.

Disha looked confused for a moment and later realised that it was the same guy who held her when the ball hit her. She blushed as she remembered his touch, his face up close, and his fragrance, which she realised was the same one she could sense now.

"Haha, yeah, it is fine. It was really embarrassing being knocked off by a ball," Disha replied while the colour rose in her cheeks, remembering how he held her.

"Are you thinking about your past or future?" she asked, staring at the waves, trying to change the topic.

"Currently, I am thinking of the past that I had hidden in the deep layers of my brain. No matter how well you hide, the memories, even on the slightest trigger, come rushing at you with great force like these waves, only to recede, leaving traces behind," Arjun said somewhat sadly.

"I understand what you are saying. I was thinking a lot about the past, too, yesterday. But today, I feel like a different person," Disha said.

"What changed from yesterday? If I may ask?" Arjun said.

"Well, I was scared to face my past. Someone whom I loved dearly and lost for some silly reason. But once I faced him, I realised I was carrying an unnecessary burden all along. I was trying to make him a villain in my life. It was not worth it. I realised that I had let go of him long back; it's just a fear I had inside me, fear of being left, fear of being abandoned, has made me so weak that I wasted ten precious years of my life. I now think of it as a lesson about how to handle relationships so that I know when the right one comes or, if he doesn't, that I am enough. I think every moment of our lives is like a grain of sand. Each story is a lesson in that moment in time. They may seem insignificant, but together, they make a beach of life we stand on. Sometimes, these moments have weak links, so they try to pull you down. You only push yourself harder to take out your foot and move forward. Sometimes, you are out of breath. Sometimes, you are so tired that you have to pause and stand and recover, but you cannot stay there forever because you will sink into it. You need to move, work harder, forget the pain and make your way to your destiny. Once you make it out of the sand, you feel like you have accomplished. Many times, you tend to keep going back, but now your feet are accustomed, and they know the way out. If your memories are coming to you, let them. Don't let them weigh you down. Once you understand how to navigate, they will stop becoming the hindrance and will become a fun place to be in," Asha said.

ॐ That Fateful Day ☙

Arjun turned to look at her, his eyes reflecting a mix of nostalgia and wisdom. "And also like the ocean," he added. "Our past is vast and deep, some mysteries, some wonders. Some parts are turbulent, and others are beautiful, but everything is required to make it whole."

"Agreed," Disha said.

But the pain Arjun felt is way beyond words. That day could have ended differently. Asha and Arjun would have been at a different level if that day didn't happen.

Arjun closed his eyes, and the tears found a way to escape despite his attempts to erase the pain. He quickly dried them up, noticing Disha watching the waves.

"It is ok to let them flow, you know. Sometimes, it helps you let go of what is holding you back. I am telling you from my experience. The more you hold back, the more you will question yourself and the more you will hurt. Some whys cannot be answered. It's like how our mums say, 'Because I said so,' when they don't have a right answer. Sometimes we learn only in hindsight about why something happened," Disha said.

"You are lucky; you were at least able to come face-to-face with your past and face your fears head-on. I don't have that choice. She is no more, and I lost her because of me. I wish I could turn back time and not do what I did. I wish I hadn't planned that big proposal; she would have been alive, and maybe we would have been happily married and had kids by now," Arjun said, gulping down the pain in his voice.

"I am sorry to hear that. But I believe you should let go of her. You should let her rest in peace. The hardest part in life is forgiving yourself. Forgiving yourself for not thinking through. I know she can't come back, but you need to let her go. She is in a safe place. She would not want to see you sad, isn't it? Life is precious, Arjun. You might have a lot of people in your life who have been wanting to see you happy. I am not saying you should forget and move on for those around you, but since you already lost someone close, hold on to those around you preciously. Make your life worth living and be happy. No amount of sadness or grief will change the past. Time doesn't come back, and we only get one chance at life and sometimes a second one, like the one I feel I have now that my mind is clear. Life is beautiful; live it to the fullest. I hope I didn't intrude by saying this," Disha said.

"Hmmm," Arjun responded, with tears flowing.

Both continued staring at the waves, each thinking of their own world.

As they sat there immersed in their own thoughts, they heard the sound of whistles blowing, asking everyone to leave. Both got back to their feet, smiled, and started to go back.

"Disha!" Arjun called. "Would you like to go around Goa with me?"

"Sure," Disha said and walked back.

Back in the room, Arjun pondered over what Disha said. She struck a chord with him. It is not that he didn't know all of this, but throughout his life, he only came across people trying to steer away from him or letting him be. He never spoke about Asha to anyone. People understood his pain and anger. They didn't say anything. Talking to Disha felt different. She seemed to have been through the path of losing someone closer. She knows what she is saying because she has been through the journey.

Arjun kept thinking about Asha and fell asleep, tears rolling from his eyes.

CHAPTER 8

EXPLORING THE CITY TOGETHER

Disha reached her room and thought about the new version of Arjun she saw. She felt a strange connection with him. He was so vulnerable, with so much pain, unlike the strong man she saw the other day. She felt like he was struggling with unresolved emotions, and she felt like being there for him. She wanted to console him.

Generally, she would have said no to anyone who would have asked to go around. She never trusted anyone, but Arjun shared his vulnerable moment inadvertently, and she got to see the man. She wanted to know more about him. She felt like she would be safe with him; at the same time, she felt like protecting him.

She wondered how the day would unfold. She shared her contact information with Arjun before coming back.

"Will he reach out, or will he feel embarrassed to contact again?" she thought.

Disha drifted to sleep, thinking of taking one day at a time, as she had promised herself. She will enjoy her life and live every day as it comes by.

As dawn broke, a soft palette of orange and pink hues painted the Goan sky, signalling the start of an adventurous day ahead.

Disha got up, got ready, and decided to have her breakfast and then to head out and explore on her own if Arjun doesn't message her.

She kept thinking back to last night, how the tears were rolling off his cheeks. She resisted the temptation to look at him and console him. She tried to remain neutral, but through the night, she kept wondering if he was feeling okay.

Just as she finished her breakfast, Arjun came to the area and said, "Good morning."

She looked up and smiled.

Arjun smiled back.

"I was unsure of when you would wake up and didn't want to wake you up myself. I thought of first having breakfast and then calling you. Luckily, you are here. I should have given my number to you. I wasn't thinking right yesterday. Sorry if I kept you wondering," he said politely.

Disha was surprised at how simply he stated the facts.

"He seems to be a very straightforward person. No beating around the bush, so good," she thought.

ꘓ Exploring the City Together ꘒ

"Yeah, no worries. I am an early riser. I was wondering the same. I was planning to explore myself if you don't reach out, so no worries," Disha said.

"Cool, then it's settled. Let me grab some breakfast."

It was the first time for Disha to be in Goa, so she asked Arjun to take the lead.

Arjun decided to take her on the regular hangouts first and then explore the unknowns of Goa, depending on her appetite.

They first went around the regular beaches like Calangute, Anjuna, and Arambol. Disha mentioned she had already been to Baga. Then, they visited the famous Chapora Fort, which became famous due to the movie "Dil Chahta Hai."

Disha jumped with happiness and looked around like a child who was given a free pass. Arjun enjoyed watching her. While Disha kept looking around, Arjun took out his camera and started taking the photos. He was an avid photographer but lost touch due to all his running away.

Arjun felt a lump in his throat for the first click. He remembered the very first time he held a camera. His mum took him around the garden and made him snap pictures of whatever he thought was beautiful. That was how his observation skills developed. He used to run around the garden to look for something beautiful; then, he started observing unique things. Some of his pictures included colourful flowers, dried leaves, and sometimes even cracks in the walls. He started loving nature for its abundance in everything.

"Will you take my picture, please? I always wanted some candid ones," Disha asked.

"Sure, why not? You keep exploring, and I will keep taking your pictures," Arjun said.

Disha smiled, beaming.

"She is so cute," Arjun thought and continued taking pictures.

They then decided to look for the places less travelled and to explore the lesser-known gems of Goa, away from the crowded beaches and bustling markets.

The first stop was The Cube Gallery in Moira. The architectural wonder was a space where contemporary art blended seamlessly with nature. The structure, made primarily of laterite stones, was a maze of tiny rooms, courtyards, and staircases. As they wandered through the exhibits, a particular installation caught their attention: a series of mirrors positioned to reflect the surrounding greenery in an infinite loop. It was as if the artist had captured a piece of the Goan wilderness inside a room.

After a quick brunch of sannas and sorpotel, a local Goan delicacy, at a nearby café, they headed to Netravali Bubbling Lake in Sanguem. The mystery of the lake lay in the bubbles that popped up spontaneously. Locals believed that clapping or creating vibrations near the lake led to an increase in bubbles. Intrigued, Disha clapped her hands, and Arjun laughed heartily at her childish expression, hoping to see the bubbles. Legends spoke of a subterranean connection to the sea, but the exact reason for this phenomenon remained an enigma.

The sun climbed higher, and the duo decided to find some respite from the heat. They drove to the Lamgau Caves in Bicholim. These ancient Buddhist caves, carved out of laterite, told stories of times long past. Exploring the insides, they found chambers with tiny windows allowing streaks of sunlight to enter, creating an ethereal play of light and shadow.

As evening approached, Disha and Arjun decided to witness a Goan secret - the Tiracol Fort. Located at the northern tip of Goa, this fort offered panoramic views of the Arabian Sea. While the fort itself was a historical masterpiece, the real surprise awaited at the hidden beach just below. The beach, accessible only during low tide, was a serene expanse of golden sand with not a soul in sight. They sat there, watching the sun dip into the horizon, the waves playing a soft lullaby.

The final destination was the secluded Kakolem Beach, a hidden cove reachable through a challenging trek down a steep cliff. The beach was a haven of tranquillity, untouched by commercialisation. The gushing sound of a hidden waterfall nearby and the rhythmic collision of waves against the rocks composed a harmonious melody, creating a symphony of solitude. This beach felt like the secret end of the world, a place where the sands of time stood still.

For dinner, they visited Gunpowder in Assagao. This quirky eatery, housed in a Portuguese villa, served a mix of Goan and South Indian cuisines. With its eclectic decor and lush gardens, it was a fitting end to their unusual day in Goa.

As they drove back to their accommodation, the vibrant, lesser-known side of Goa left an indelible mark on their hearts.

The next day, Disha woke up early, eager to know what the next places they could visit. Arjun did not reveal the plan for the next day, but yesterday was so good that the traveller and the explorer in Disha are eager to see and learn more about Goa.

CHAPTER 9

THE BEGINNING OF A NEW CHAPTER

Arjun felt happy after a very long time. Going around with Disha was refreshing. He had been living a mechanical life for a very long time, and for the first time in his life, he felt like he was breathing freely. He felt alive, and he felt like living. Disha is very sweet and somehow calms down everything around her.

The next day, Arjun planned to take Disha around South Goa. They made plans to start very early. Old Goa is known for its finely constructed churches and the culture that it follows. They first visited one of the most historical sites, Cabo De Rama. Arjun was curious to see if Disha gets excited like yesterday, but this time, she didn't act as before; she seemed more composed, mindful, and enjoying calmly. Then, they visited the Mahadev temple, and Disha seemed interested in the architecture. She didn't look so eager today.

Next, Arjun decided to take her to the beaches. He chose very unique beaches to go to. He took her to Betalbatim Beach, which has clean white sand and serene surroundings. He saw Disha's smile widen.

"Ah, she loves beaches over forts and mountains," Arjun thought and smiled.

Arjun added a few more beaches to the list of places to visit. He took her to the Hollant beach and Talpona beach, both very serene and calm. The beaches did work their wonders for Arjun as well. They walked along the beach, silently lost in thoughts. Arjun didn't notice Disha falling behind, and he turned back when she yelled his name.

He felt a tingling sensation all over when she called his name, a feeling he is not used to. He turned back to see Disha trying to pull something out of her leg. He ran back to her, and it was a tiny crab clutching onto her finger. Disha had tears in her eyes as she pulled it out.

Arjun gently held her foot, examining the small red mark where the crab had pinched her. "Looks like you've made a fierce little enemy," he joked, his touch sending an unexpected shiver up her spine. He helped her to a nearby rock where they sat side by side, and Arjun continued to make sure she was alright, his care for her clear and unwavering.

They sat there, and Arjun got her some cold water. They both sat for a while, watching the waters. As the sky darkened

The Beginning of a New Chapter

and the first star made its appearance, Arjun wrapped his jacket around Disha as it started to get colder. Disha stared at him, enjoying the closeness and the warmth. Arjun also felt different. He felt like this was no longer an innocent trip with a stranger. He started liking her. He wanted to know more about her. He realised that throughout the day, he had been trying to understand what she likes and how she acts in certain situations. He started to adapt to her.

Disha couldn't brush off how she felt when Arjun touched her foot. She could sense the delicateness with which he held her as if she would break if he let her go. When he helped her to the rock, she was acutely aware of his arm around her waist and how gently he held her. He was so strong. She felt a desire to be close to him. She wanted more of him.

Arjun asked if Disha wanted to eat anything.

Disha said no.

Arjun said, "Disha, I want to know more about you. Would you like to tell me your story?"

Disha wasn't expecting this question, but then she told him all that happened and about how she coped in life, her stages of depression, how she came across Ananya, and all her friends.

Arjun just kept listening to her, trying to understand how her life had been. He felt very angry towards Varun. He held Disha as tears rolled down her eyes. Disha rested her head on Arjun's shoulder and kept staring at the sea as her tears left her.

After some time, Disha realised he had been resting on Arjun for quite some time and immediately lifted her head, only to see Arjun staring into her eyes. She quickly moved a bit, and that broke the eye contact.

"Let us start walking if you feel good," suggested Arjun.

"Yes, I think the pain has subsided. I can walk now," said Disha, getting up.

They started walking back to the bike.

"Now that you know about me, it is only fair that you tell me your story. Why were you so upset and sad yesterday? I really wanted to ask you, but I felt you needed your space. Can you share something about you with me?" Disha asked.

Arjun sighed and said, "Yes, I can share my story."

He told about Asha and how they met. All the lovely things they did and how he lost her. He also told her how they were planning to get married and how they had everything planned to the detail. He told her about how he left the country and how this is the first time he is returning after years.

Arjun had tears in his eyes too. Disha looked at him and felt like she wants to take care of him and protect him. She turned to him and hugged him. Arjun was surprised by this,

༺ The Beginning of a New Chapter ༻

and he hugged her back. He just closed his eyes as his tears found their way out. Disha held on to him a bit longer.

It started drizzling a bit, bringing both to the present. Both of them rushed to the bike.

They got on the bike and started to go back to the hotel, and it started raining heavily. Disha held on to Arjun tightly, hugging him. She held onto his t-shirt tightly, and she could feel the heat rise in her body. Arjun drove faster to avoid the rain, but he was clearly aware of what Disha was doing to him. As he continued driving, Disha clutched him tighter and hid her face behind his back.

The rain was relentless, and it was impossible to drive on the two-wheeler. So, Arjun decided to stop at a nearby place. He called the bike rental company, told them about the situation, and shared his location. The bike rental guy was kind enough to let them leave the bike there and find a car to reach their destination.

Arjun held Disha's hand and ran towards the nearby house for shelter.

CHAPTER 10

HIDDEN DESIRES

Disha and I ran to take shelter from the rain. The typical feelings you experience, when you are with a beautiful girl, started taking shape in my brain. The urge to get closer to her seems to be more.

I suddenly longed for companionship. The hidden emotions started to rise, the craving to be closer to someone, for someone who understands my pain yet brings a glimmer of hope. She seems to be that hope, her presence a balm to my tired soul.

Yet, the fear of opening my heart once more, only to be shattered again, started to stir. As the thoughts kept swarming in my mind, the need to hug her started to rise. She seemed to feel the closeness as well, but she kept staring at the rain. I think maybe she is unsure of what to do as well. There is a warm feeling I get with her, and I am sure it is mutual.

As in movies, there was a cliché moment. A car that went through was speeding and splashing all the water, giving no care to those walking. Disha moved a step back and bumped into me. With an instinct, I opened my arms to hold her. The warmth from her body seeped into mine. It felt nice. She moved deeper into my arms instead of away, signalling the same. I closed my arms around her from the back, holding her in a warm embrace. We were standing so close that the warmth of the body heat started to be more intoxicating with the coldness and the dampness around us. I kept contemplating more on what was going on in my brain. I kept feeling emotions I thought I lost; the weight of my past began to lift, replaced by a sense of peace. Perhaps she's the answer to my prayers, a beacon of light in my darkness.

We stood together in silence, two souls bound by loss and longing. In embracing her, I felt a kind of solace.

We stood like that for what felt like an eternity and regained clarity with the car honk. Our ride was here.

Disha rushed to get into the car, and I followed her lead. As we walked hand in hand, I didn't want to let go of her. I wanted her badly.

I sat with her in the seat and moved closer to avoid getting drenched. Our bodies touched each other. Neither of us moved away. It was as if something would break if we did. We sat stiff and still, enjoying each other's warmth. I could sense she was a bit apprehensive, and I could see her fiddling with her hair and clutching her bag tight. I knew that, at that moment, she was waiting for me to take the lead. She was hesitant, not moving away from me. I put my arm around her and brought her closer. She didn't resist. I shifted to make room for her.

The rain tapped against the windscreen like a soft melody, creating a cocoon of intimacy within the confines of the car. We sat in comfortable silence, the only sound accompanying us being the rhythmic swish of the windscreen wipers.

As the rain poured outside, I stole glances at her, the droplets clinging to her hair shining like stars. Her eyes held a mix of calmness and longing like the rain had stirred something deep inside her.

I reached out to gently brush a stray lock of hair from her face, feeling the warmth of her skin beneath my fingertips. Our eyes met, and in that fleeting moment, a silent understanding passed between us – a recognition of the unspoken bond that was about to bind our hearts together.

The air between us crackled with anticipation, charged with the electricity of unspoken desires. And as the rain continued to fall, we surrendered ourselves to its embrace, letting it wash away the barriers that had kept us apart.

In the soft glow of the dashboard lights, I leaned in closer, my breath mingling with hers in the confined space of the car. Our lips met in a tender kiss, a meeting of souls amidst the chaos of the storm.

And as we melted into each other's embrace, the rain served as a backdrop to our yet-to-start love story – a testament to the raw beauty of our connection, unyielding in the face of adversity. At that moment, we were two souls intertwined, finding solace in the shelter of each other's arms as the world outside faded into obscurity.

As our kiss lingered, the sound of a passing car jolted us back to reality. We pulled away, but the warmth of our connection lingered in the air between us. There was a sense of reluctance in our movements as if we both wished to stay lost in the moment a little while longer.

The car rumbled on, its fading sound echoing in the distance, growing between us and the outside world. Inside the car, however, a different distance emerged – not physical, but emotional. We both retreated into our thoughts, grappling with the intensity of the moment we had just shared. Uncertainty mingled with desire, and as the rain continued to fall, we found ourselves in an unfamiliar world, unsure of where it would lead us next.

The atmosphere inside the car felt charged with anticipation, as if we were both waiting for something to happen but unsure of what it might be.

Finally, the headlights illuminated the sign of our destination. As we pulled into the parking lot, a sense of relief washed over me, mingled with a hint of nervousness. It was as if the arrival at the hotel marked the beginning of a new chapter, one filled with unknown possibilities.

We stepped out of the car, the cool rain refreshing against our skin. We made our way to the entrance, the glow of the lobby beckoning us inside. Our minds are still reeling from the intensity of the moments shared in the car.

Disha looked up at me as we walked, questioning what was about to happen next.

"Your room?" I asked as I knew mine was definitely filled with my friends. She nodded and led the way.

As we made our way to our room, the nervous energy that had accompanied us seemed to dissipate, replaced by a sense of calm anticipation.

It continued to rain outside, the slow sound nudging and creating an atmosphere. It felt as though the world outside had faded away, leaving just the two of us in our own little zone.

Disha started clearing out the stuff around the room. I chuckled and went behind her, hugged her from behind. She froze, unsure, and rather anticipating what is about to happen.

I turned her around, kissed her forehead, then her eyes, and slowly moved to her lips. I know what I want, but I hesitate if she wants the same too. She moved forward, signalling that she wanted the same, and I kissed her slowly and tenderly, exploring the corners of her mouth and teasing with her lips. I can feel the heat rising inside me. I tried hard to stay in control, but my body seemed to have a mind of its own. I kissed her passionately and gently, and she held onto me tightly as we got closer.

We struggled through our clothes as they were too wet and fell down laughing. I picked her up and landed on her on the bed, and we made passionate love, very slowly trying to know each other, the points, the turn-ons, and the contours of each other's bodies. We became one.

Lying on the bed, we looked at each other, a silent understanding passing between us. It was as if we both knew that this moment was significant, a turning point in our relationship.

And as we leaned in to kiss once more, the world outside disappeared, leaving just the two of us in our own little bubble of intimacy. The rain continued to fall outside, but inside, the warmth of our embrace, we found solace amidst the storm.

Disha woke up in the middle of the night feeling thirsty. Suddenly, she realised she was with Arjun and their clothes were everywhere but on them. She turned to look at Arjun. He was sleeping peacefully but was snoring so cutely. She wondered if she was snoring as well. Her body began to ache. She got up to drink water and looked at the mirror. There were love bites all over.

"We were too passionate," she thought, blushing. What is going to happen next? She pondered.

She felt lighter and happier. The last few days with Arjun have been wonderful. It did not feel as if she met him for the first time; it felt like they belonged together as if they were destined to meet. Her thoughts went on seamlessly, and they broke off when she heard Arjun move. She smiled and went back to bed. Arjun put his hand around her, dragged her close, and hugged her.

"What took you so long to come back?" he asked drowsily.

"Gosh, he sounds so sexy in that voice," thought Disha.

"Did I wake you up? Sorry," Disha said.

Arjun opened his eyes slightly and looked at her.

"Yes, you woke me up, and you will be punished for that. You have awakened the monster inside me, and now you will have to suffer," he said. Saying that, he started kissing her all over, making her giggle.

"Ah, my lady is ticklish," he said as he got the realisation.

"Please don't," begged Disha amidst giggles.

"Ah, too late," Arjun said and started tickling her.

Disha kept trying to get away, and Arjun held her on. As tears were almost running down her eyes, he stopped, moved close to her, hugged her, and kissed her.

"You are so beautiful. Your laugh is enticing. I feel like making you laugh all the time. I love hearing you laugh," said Arjun, kissing her again.

"I have lots to say, but some other time. Hug me closer now," said Disha.

Arjun moved closer and started to kiss her passionately.

"I said hug, not kiss, in between the moments," said Disha.

"Sorry, I suddenly have a hearing problem," said Arjun, continuing to kiss Disha.

Both of them explored each other, this time slowly trying to get to know each other. Arjun noticed a few points in Disha, which he mentally noted down, intending to make the best use of them in the future, with a smile.

Disha felt the warmth of being with Arjun. She felt like she was safe with him, a kind of gut feeling that he knew and understood her. Even when they hardly knew each other, she didn't feel like he was someone new. She felt like lost souls met each other finally. The way they know and are able to understand each other doesn't happen just like that.

Thinking that, Disha slowly drifted to sleep in Arjun's arms.

Arjun kept staring at her for a very long time until he finally fell asleep.

Next morning, Disha woke up to Arjun kissing her. She suddenly remembered what they did last night and blushed, pulling the blanket over her face.

"You can't do that," said Arjun, pulling her blanket away.

"I like the Disha I met last night. The shy one won't work," said Arjun, kissing her again.

"Mm, I just got up. Let me go brush. I am feeling embarrassed," Disha said, covering her mouth.

"Sorry darling, I can't wait so long," said Arjun, kissing her all over and sucking her breasts, making her cry in pleasure. Arjun kept kissing her deeply and made love to her. Disha matched his wavelength perfectly, and they made love for what felt like an eternity.

After an hour or so, Disha got up to freshen up, and after some time, Arjun joined her in the shower. Disha pushed him to go away, feeling shy. Arjun held her arms and pushed her back to the wall. He looked into her eyes and asked, "Do you really want me to go?"

Disha nodded her head, saying, "Yes,"

"Are you sure?" Arjun asked, kissing her on her neck.

"Mmm," said Disha.

"Is that an answer to the kiss or the answer to my questions?" asked Arjun.

"Both," said Disha, pushing Arjun out of the shower.

CHAPTER 11
DOUBTS AND CHALLENGES

"The one week they had in Goa went away so fast. Shall we stay back," asked Arjun while Disha was rushing to pack.

"I wish, but Ananya will be alone, and mum will start to worry," sighed Disha.

"Well, we can meet in Mumbai, right?" asked Disha, knowing fully well that the answer is going to be different.

"I need to go back to the US; my work is there, Disha," Arjun said with a lump in his throat, realising the realities of life they need to face.

"So, is this it? Is this like what happens in Goa stays in Goa?" Disha said, turning away to avoid him seeing the tears in her eyes.

"No, silly. Is that what you think of me, Disha? After all that we experienced here, do you really think that?" Arjun said, sounding hurt.

I am not a player. I have never been with anyone before, and I don't think I will be after I met you. I know a week is a short time to decide, but I know for sure that you are what I need in my life. I have a special bond with you, and I don't want to lose you. I have come across lots of girls after Asha, but I never let anyone close to me because I didn't want to get hurt again. With you, it is different. I feel like I want to be with you, I want to protect you, I want to see you smile, and I want to stand by you. It is too early to feel all this. I don't have all the answers now, but I want you with me on this journey. I am not the one to hurt anyone, Disha because I know how it feels not to be able to talk to the one you love. I know it all too well," said Arjun, with a painful memory coming up.

"It's very hard. I need to know. I don't want to keep waiting. I did that once before, and Varun left me. He ghosted me. I can't go through it all again. If it happens again, then I will not be able to survive it. I stayed away from all this for so long because the hurt was painful. I don't have that kind of energy this time. I will crumble. So, I am scared to have a relationship, and that is a long-distance one. It makes me go through that restlessness. I cannot deal with the insecurity and helplessness," said Disha.

"Yes, it is not going to be easy, Disha. Still, we can't ignore what we are feeling on the inside. I like you, and I can feel that. But I cannot stay here in India as my work is in the US. I have built a life there. There is so much to do and so much

༄ Doubts and Challenges ༈

to explore. I prefer to live there. There is more to life there than here," Arjun said.

"I do not agree with it. I want to stay in India," said Disha with tears in her eyes.

"India is good in every way. Our mums are getting older; they need enough support and medical care. Ananya has all her friends here. All my friends are here. They have been the biggest support system for me. I never had to worry about anything as I know they've got my back. I don't want to restart my life in an unknown world. I know I am looking out for my comforts, Arjun, but these people are my comfort. They took care of me through my worst, and I want to be there for them. I will be unhappy if I leave everything and go. This is not what I want to do. I really like you, and I want to be with you, but I love them all too, and I want to be there for them when they need me, and I can't do it from a distance. I don't want to live a life where I am counting money or checking for cheaper flights when I need to see someone. I can't live like that. I will suffocate," said Disha.

"I don't know what to say," said Arjun, pausing for a moment.

"Can we not overthink at this moment? We met each other just a few days back. I want to know more about you. I want to be able to explore our relationship. I want to know if you can handle me. I want to know about Ananya. There is a lot I want to do. This is not a fling, Disha. I want you, and I want to make lots of love to you," saying that Arjun moved close to Disha, hugged her in a warm embrace, gently pushed her to bed, and started kissing her.

Disha kissed Arjun back and felt the warmth of his hug. She felt safe with him. There is no uncertainty in her mind. She wants to explore life with him. She will not let the past scars ruin her life. Just because someone died in a car crash doesn't mean she will never travel. Though that someone is her in this case, she needs to move away from the past and show up in the present. Arjun is caring, and it might be impossible to decide what's next and the entire future now. He is also trying to figure out his life. He needs to make sense of what he wants in life and what he can adjust to.

"I cannot just bombard into his life and manipulate his thinking. He needs to get to decide his life for himself. I have special feelings for him. I want him in my life. I think we will be great together, and Ananya will also love him. I don't know what the future holds but let me not ruin this moment. Let me take one step at a time," thought Disha and leaned closer to Arjun.

Both of them behaved as if there were no tomorrow, aiming to make the best of each moment together. The way they touch each other is laced with lots of emotions. There is a fine balance of rawness and gentleness in the way they caress each other. Every gesture, every touch, and every glance is an expression of deep-seated desire and feelings. Amidst the chaos in their minds, they found solace in each other's

Doubts and Challenges

warmth, embracing and driving each other to the edge as if there were no tomorrow.

The call from reception brought them back to reality.

Disha finished packing her bags, and Arjun took her to the cab. They went to the airport, and Arjun bid her goodbye as she left to go into the airport. Arjun went back to the hotel with his friends. He continued to spend more time in Goa, thinking about Disha.

Disha boarded the flight and sat in her seat. This trip has been nothing like what she thought and everything that she needed. She had closure with Varun, something she never thought would happen in her lifetime, and then she met Arjun, someone she never thought would come into her life. Her mind felt clear, and she was radiant from within.

As soon as she landed, Disha rushed home to her daughter and mum.

Disha opened up her baggage and showed Ananya all the stuff she bought for her. Ananya loved them, especially the t-shirt which Arjun chose for her.

As Ananya went on looking through the stuff, Disha went to her mum and hugged her.

"Love you lots, maa," she said.

Disha's mum looked at her daughter and said, "I am happy for you."

Disha blushed. Her mum understood everything, even when she didn't utter a word. Mum's love is always out of this world; they seem to know when to do what.

Disha messaged in the group, "Girls, I am back."

CHAPTER 12
WITH THE GIRLS

"Where are we meeting?" Gayathri's message popped up.

"I am ready and waiting forever," Nisha responded.

"Shall we meet at the coffee place we go to?" asked Disha.

"No way, come to my place. I am alone and need to do lots of house cleaning. Come over, and we can have a girls' slumber party where you help me clean, and I cook for you," said Shriya.

"Fine, let's meet at your place then," Shriya, Disha replied.

As soon as Disha reached, Shriya, Gayatri, and Nisha came and hugged her.

Shriya switched on some music and then got all the snacks out. Settling down near the sofa, she started, "Now, give us all the details."

"Well, I told you about Varun. I got really scared when I came across him at the airport. I literally ran away to the washrooms, which, as you know, are the only places he cannot follow. It took me a while to calm myself down. I was super shocked. I wasn't expecting to see him ever again. I felt like my heart would burst out for a moment. It was beating so fast. I felt he looked as handsome as ever. Actually, even better now, I would say," said Disha.

"Please don't go back to him. Don't forget how he treated you and how much time you spent on getting over your depression," Gayatri said.

"No babes. I am never going back. Like I said on the phone. The chapter is closed. I got my closure already. I guess I was holding on to the anger. I was angry that I trusted him, and I was angry that he didn't feel that I was important enough to discuss his big decision. He just left as if I was just some random time pass. I was hurt, and I felt like this is not how you treat your love. It took me time to accept the fact that he never loved me. Anyway, back to the present. I felt a surge of anger and all the emotions. I thought of coming back home, but then I remembered that you all worked so hard to get me going, and I didn't want to look foolish and wonder what if. I didn't want to run away. I wanted to face what I was feeling. I sat there in the washroom, unable to get out. I was wondering whether he was still waiting outside for me. I was scared, really scared that I would lose it all, and I would beg him or demand him. I really didn't know what to do next. But then, I calmed down.

"I thought, wait, why does he get to trigger me like that? He can only play the part I decide for him to play in my life. In my life, he made a decision that rattled me and made me feel the most vulnerable of all time. Now, this Disha is different. She has learnt her lesson. She decided to make the best of her life, and one more decision she needed to make was that I decided I should go about my life. He is just another passenger in the airport and in my life. He left. That is something I need to remember."

"That's my Disha," said Gayatri, sounding a bit relieved.

Disha chuckled, wondering how the girls would react to the whole story.

"Please continue," Nisha said.

"So I went back and boarded the plane. I was so scared, and my heart was beating so fast. I just didn't know what I should say if I came across him again. However, I thought it was just a breeze of connection from the past and that I should not read much into it. I went to my seat and sat there. Then I saw Varun boarding the flight. I got so scared. I was sure now he was going to talk to me. I don't know what to say. Just like in movies, he came and sat next to me," Disha paused after saying it.

"What?" Shriya screamed.

"Why so much suspense, tell us what happened next?" Nisha said.

"Ok, ok. So, he sat next to me, and I acted as if I had slept off because I didn't want to talk to him. He did try to talk, but I just closed my eyes tight. Literally, the whole flight, I was just closing my eyes in fear. Then, once we landed, I literally ran out of the airport. I was standing for the cab, and the cab driver looked so scary. Varun asked if he could join me. I said yes out of fear," I replied.

"Why did you say yes? I am pretty sure you had to ask him all your stupid questions. That's why, right?" Gayatri asked.

"Yes, I was not sure, but I had plenty of questions. But mainly, I was too scared to go alone in the cab that day," I replied.

"What happened in the cab?" Nisha asked.

"Nothing much, I told the rest to you. I closed my eyes, and once we reached our destination, he followed me. He asked for a room in the hotel. Then I realised he just followed me randomly and he didn't have a plan to come to Goa. I told him he could share my room until he found one. We went to the room. I was tensed and nervous. I didn't know why I invited him. Slowly, I realised that my mind was playing its way through. I have nothing to conclude. He took a decision, and I suffered a consequence. There was nothing more to it. A decade is a long time to find someone. He did not make an attempt to. So, all is well. He decided to leave, and I decided to let go of the anger." said Disha.

"So, did he leave immediately? Why did you stay so long? Was he there for the whole time? Tell the juicy parts," Shriya said.

"Oh god, just shut up," Gayatri said.

"Actually, there are juicy parts to the story," Disha said sheepishly.

"No way," said Nisha.

"Listen now," said Disha.

Gayatri started looking upset at what she might have to hear next.

"Well, after Varun left, I went for a walk on the beach, and I felt very calm as if there was a heavyweight that was lifted off my shoulders. I heard someone calling out, and when I turned around, a ball hit squarely on my face. I was just about to fall down, and then someone held me. He smelled awesome, his voice was damn sexy, and he had strong hands. I was about to touch his face and then suddenly got to my senses," Disha paused and blushed, looking at the expression on their faces.

"What happened next?" Gayatri literally screamed.

Disha blushed even more.

"I ran away from the place," Disha replied.

"Did you meet him again?" Shriya asked eagerly.

"Yes, I came across him again multiple times, and then we met. We spoke about ourselves, and then we went all over Goa on a bike, and we made out," said Disha, hiding her face.

"No way," screamed Shriya.

"Idiot, you said that stupid Varun story in detail, but you are finishing this one in a single sentence. We are not letting this slide. We need all the details right now," Gayatri said, getting all excited.

All the girls moved closer, and Disha hid her face, blushing even more.

"Tell me," Nisha also asked.

So, Disha told the entire story, every minute part of it. When she shared the details of their lovemaking with the girls, she started missing Arjun.

Disha wondered if he would reach out again, or if he will leave for the US.

She was unsure.

Gayatri kept looking at Disha, noticing how animated she was when she spoke about Arjun, but she knew in her heart how scared Disha was about the whole thing.

"I just hope this guy won't hurt her and treat her the way she deserves to be treated, like a queen." Thought Gayathri.

The girls went crazy over the story, and they spent the entire day giggling and laughing.

With the Girls

Disha felt so happy. This time she had someone to share about herself. She is not alone, and she is less scared and more prepared in case the history repeats itself. Nothing hurts more than wiping your own tears, knowing that you can't tell anyone about the things you were crying about.

Gayatri came and hugged Disha. Sometimes, all you need is a person who can understand your unsaid words and emotions.

"I am scared," Disha whispered to Gayatri.

"I understand, but you know what? You should remember the three C's of life - Choices, Chances, and Changes. You must make a choice to take a chance, or your life will never change."

"I know you never found time to be really happy because you were always forced to be strong by your circumstances, but I am wishful that it will change this time."

"Do you think this is temporary? I really like him. I wish he was for real, but I am too scared to ask for much. I am trying to live in the present and accept what I get. A little bit of love also feels like a lot," Disha said.

"You know, sometimes such interactions end up being lifetime commitments. I am not going to encourage or discourage you, but I will definitely cheer for you. I always wanted you to find yourself and find someone who realises your worth. Do remember one thing: everyone in your life will have a last day with you, and you won't know when it will be. Just don't get hurt by them leaving you, and live your life as if there is no tomorrow," Gayatri said.

Disha hugged her in silence. This time, she is happy, and she has found someone whom she wants in her life.

CHAPTER 13

GETTING BACK HOME

I landed in Mumbai and went home directly.

Mum hugged me and cried. I went to her after 8 years. She couldn't control her tears anymore.

"I am sorry, Ma. Please forgive me. I will never leave you alone like this again. I made a huge mistake. I was selfish, and I should have looked beyond myself. I am really sorry that I took so long," I said with tears welling up in my eyes.

Mum just hugged me knowingly. "I understand, beta, but I missed you terribly," she said.

"Coffee or tea?" Mum asked.

"Hungry, mum, can I eat something?" I said.

"Yaa, your favourite Rajma Chawal is ready. Go freshen up and come," mum said.

"Love you, mum," I said and went to my room.

Mum seems to have refreshed the room. The decor has changed, and everything seems to be very pleasing and suits my preferences.

Once I had freshened up, I went to the kitchen and hugged mum.

"I am really sorry, mum. I will make it up to you. I shouldn't have done what I did. I was too selfish. I am really sorry," I said.

"It's ok, beta. I understand you were grieving, and there was so much on your mind, but I didn't expect that you would be affected so much by it. I do understand it was the biggest blow ever. I wish you'd let me in and help you out, but again, sometimes, we have to deal with our own demons. So, I get it," mum said.

"Gosh, you are so understanding. I just love you, mum. Since you did all the cooking, I will do all the cleaning," I said.

"Did you think I have all the energy to do it all? I am getting older. I am waiting to retire and rest," said mum.

I never thought of it. I looked at her. She looks a lot older and frail. Somehow, I only have the version of my young, energetic mum who was always there for me. I felt like mum always did everything. I never cared about what she would like to do or what she wanted from life. It's like you always assume that your parents will do anything for you and there is nothing you need to do for them.

I was so involved with my own suffering, with my own life, that I never looked at her. I never spent a moment with her. She always shielded her pain from me, or rather, I never looked at her to see her pain.

I feel like an idiot, not caring at all about mum.

I decided that I needed to take better care of mum. I should make sure that she is happy. I will take her back with me and make sure that I provide her with everything she deserves. She shouldn't be living alone when I am there.

As we finished our dinner, mum and I sat in our favourite place, and mum started massaging my hair, just like in old times. I told her all about the work, the places I visited in the US, what I liked, and all the office jokes, and mum patiently listened and smiled.

I looked at her with a questioning face, and she asked, "What's her name?"

"Mommmm," I said.

"I am happy to see you happy, beta. I have been waiting to see that smile back on your face. It's been very long," she said.

"Mum, I feel guilty to be happy. I feel like I am wronging Asha by finding someone," I said.

"You need to understand that it is not your mistake. She fulfilled her term on the earth, and she left us. There is nothing you can do about it. It is just that you were a witness to it. Life works in mysterious ways. The people who are left behind keep wondering if they did something wrong, that the one they love so much is taken away from them. Trust me. I questioned myself on the same for many years. I still wonder if things would have been different if your father were alive. Fate works in different ways. Life is unpredictable, and that's the best part about it. Enough about the past; tell me all about what you are doing, whom you met, and what is going on in your life.

"Mum, not now," said Arjun.

"Yes, now. Do you realise how long I have been waiting for you to open up? I am dying to know what is going on in your life and who that girl you met in Goa is. Tell me more about her," mum said.

"Did you speak to Vivek already? This is not fair, mum. You always talk to him first as if I hid things from you. You will never change. Anyway, I am excelling at my work. They sent me here to set up a new team, and I might get promoted soon after I fix the team here. Now coming to Disha..." Arjun said.

Arjun paused a moment and looked at his mum; her eyes were so eager to know about the girl.

Arjun smiled and said, "I saw Disha at the airport, and there were many coincidences in our meeting. First, I crashed into her at the airport, then I saw her on the same plane to Goa, then I hit her with the volleyball in her face, and then I saved her from dogs," Arjun said with a chuckle.

"You should see her, maa. She is so innocent, very delicate and possessive, but at the same time, she is so strong. When I held her after hitting her with a volleyball by mistake, all I wanted to do was to protect her. She was so phased out that I felt a kind of connection to her at that moment. It is difficult to explain, but at the same time, I felt a kind of calm, the kind..." Arjun's voice trailed off as he choked on tears.

"The kind you felt with Asha. Does this girl remind you of Asha?" Mum asked.

I hugged mum and said, "yes" and "no."

"She is lovely. She had a heartbreak a few years ago, and she went through depression. She adopted a kid who is now six years old. She is a beautiful mum. Very sensible and supportive."

There is a paradox in her strength and softness as if she is both compelling and profoundly reassuring. Her strength is not in dominance but in the clarity of her own desires and boundaries. She does not impose herself forcefully but navigates her life with quiet certainty and openness that invites others to walk alongside her rather than behind or in front of her.

Her presence is comforting and familiar, like home, rather than unpredictable and adventurous. She has a knack for understanding situations and people without needing things spelt out, knowing exactly when to offer calm, support, or take decisive action.

Her emotional intelligence is evident in her simplicity. She knows intuitively when to listen, when to support, and when to rise up and challenge. She is straightforward and unpretentious.

She is strong yet soft. She knows what she wants but is not bullish about it. She accommodates the ones around her. She is so simple yet so sophisticated. She is straightforward yet complex, showing a deep understanding of human emotions and situations. Despite being hurt in the past, which makes her cautious about whom she lets close, she offers unwavering support to those she trusts. I seem to be one of those few she lets in," Arjun said,

"Why don't you ask her to visit?" Mum asked.

"Mum, we just met. Isn't it too soon to meet her? I don't know what she wants and how she feels about me. We need to do a lot of knowing each other, you see," Arjun said.

"Fine, fine. I will wait. At least let me see her pictures. Now, don't tell me you don't have her pictures," mum said.

"Of course, I have her pictures. She loves to get candid pictures. She is just like a kid," Arjun said, showing Disha's pictures to his mum.

"She looks lovely, kind of a peaceful aura around her," mum said, checking out all her pictures.

"I know, she somehow has a calming effect," Arjun said.

"But I know the real her; she is a crazy bomb of a person. Something I love about her," Arjun thought, reminiscing their bedroom adventures.

"I need to make a call. You are going to sleep now, mum," Arjun said.

"Hello, Disha; I am back in Mumbai. What are you up to? Is it a good time to call you?" messaged Arjun.

Disha called immediately.

"Hi, Arjun; how are you? How is your mum?"

"I am good. Do you want to meet now?" asked Arjun.

"It's so late," Disha said.

"I want to see you now, please," asked Arjun.

"I can't get out of the house now," said Disha sadly.

"Send me your address; I am coming to you," said Arjun.

Arjun took out his bike and rode to Disha's place.

Disha came running to meet Arjun.

"Would you like to go on a ride with me?" asked Arjun.

"How about we go in my car?" said Disha.

"Sure," Arjun said, slightly disappointed.

"I will drive," Disha said.

Arjun found that interesting as he was always the one driving.

Disha opened the door for Arjun with a chuckle, and Arjun gave her an amused look. He moved towards the door, turned around, and Disha hugged him tightly.

Arjun hugged her back and kissed her forehead. He definitely missed her and her warmth.

"I need to keep my things in the dikki," Arjun said.

"Dikki...," laughed Disha.

"Yes, Dikki, I love your dikki too," Arjun chided her.

Disha blushed and said, "Shut up," and moved to open the back door of the car.

Arjun came behind her and hugged her again, making her feel tingling all over.

"Arjun... we are not in Goa; we are in a parking lot," Disha tried to say.

Arjun was in no mood to listen.

"Let me hug you properly. I missed you like anything," he said.

"Do you want to go on a drive or not?" Disha asked.

"Mmm, later... right now, I need you. Please don't tell me you want me to act all goody-goody," Arjun said, unable to control himself.

"Let's go upstairs," Disha said,

"What about your mum and Ananya?" Arjun asked.

"Ananya is at a sleepover, and mum is asleep," Disha said.

"Let's go then. I can't wait to kiss you properly," Arjun said.

"Shhh... you are crazy," Disha said, smiling.

As soon as Disha closed the door, Arjun held her closely and kissed her neck.

"Mmm, I missed that," Disha said.

"Let's go to my room," Disha said, pulling Arjun into her room.

"Did you miss only that... and not me," Arjun acted hurt.

Disha pushed him onto the bed, climbed on top of him, and started kissing him.

"So, I take that back; you missed me more," Arjun said, kissing her back.

Arjun turned her over and came on top, starting to kiss Disha hungrily. Disha matched his pace, and it felt as if both were treating each other to pleasure and passion. Arjun bit Disha on the neck, and she moaned so softly that it turned him on even more. He continued kissing her, giving her love bites, and Disha tried to keep her voice low. They felt like two teenagers in love, crazy and hungry for each other.

It felt as if they both belonged to each other, as if they had known each other. After making love for what felt like eternity, both hugged and slept in each other's arms. It's not just a fling, and the feelings are for real. As the past began to fade away, paving the way for new emotions and feelings, Arjun and Disha were ready to allow someone into their hearts and allow themselves to be loved.

Disha woke up in the middle of the night and kept staring at his beautiful, calm, and serene face. She wondered how this had happened. She never thought there would be someone in her life with whom she would be romantically involved. She thought her heart was closed and locked down forever, but what she is feeling now is different. She is feeling complete and content.

The next morning, Arjun and Disha woke up early. Arjun sneaked out before Disha's mum woke up. Disha felt guilty but happy. She had never done this before in her life. She felt younger as if her life had just started.

CHAPTER 14

A PACT TO FACE UNCERTAINTIES

Arjun and Disha met the next day, and they went around Mumbai. Disha showed Arjun all her favourite places, and Arjun showed her his. They went around like teenagers. Arjun's hands never left Disha's; he kept holding on to her as if she would run away if he let go. Disha enjoyed all the attention she got from him. She loved his touch and how it made her body squirm. Many times, Arjun teased her, kissed her, and did not care about the world. That made Disha blush. She would tell him not to do that in public, and he would ask if it was okay to do it in private. That would shut her up and would excite Arjun even more, knowing what she wants.

They ended up booking a hotel in the middle of the day and making out like crazy. They enjoyed each other's company. Disha would start for the office, and he would take her away with him, and they would spend the entire day and later go pick up Ananya. They had a blast throughout.

No matter how much fun they had, Disha knew this is not going to last long. The moment he leaves for the US, Arjun might even forget her, is what she thought.

Arjun kept spending as much time as possible with Disha. He knew he had to go. He was unable to understand what to do next. Was it too soon or just enough? It's been hardly a couple of days since he met Disha, but she has grown on him. He wants to spend every waking minute with her and have her close when he is sleeping, too. He understood that he not only liked Disha but also fell in love with her. It has been a while since he thought of Asha. He felt as if she had approved of his decision to make a place for love again. He felt grateful that he came across Disha. He is unsure of what Disha is thinking. He didn't want to rush her and also wanted to understand himself.

Disha is like sunshine on a rainy day. She brings out the beauty of life and fills it with rainbows. She is cute, and it takes very little to make her happy. She is adorable when she is angry and tugs at his heart when she is sad. Many times, he feels that Disha is sad and is trying hard to be normal. He wanted to ask her but also didn't want to push her. He kept waiting for her to feel free to open up to him. He knew the scars of her past, and he hoped that they were healing for her in the same way she was healing his.

A Pact to Face Uncertainties

Very soon, Arjun had to leave for the US. He and Disha met each other's families. Arjun met her friends. He understood how much everyone loved her. Arjun's mum loved Disha a lot, and she hoped that Arjun would make her his partner. However, no one wanted to touch on the subject as everyone was afraid to hurt them both.

The day has arrived, and Disha visited Arjun's home to help him pack. She was silent and kept listening to Arjun's mum, stealing glances at Arjun. Arjun was quiet, too. He didn't know what Disha felt or wanted. They never dared to speak their thoughts.

Arjun's mum understood the tension between the two and asked Disha to help Arjun pack while she finishes an errand outside.

Disha nodded and went after Arjun to his room.

As soon as they entered the room, Arjun was about to go and get his stuff when Disha hugged him from behind. Arjun felt a pain in his heart. He turned around to face her, and she hugged him even more tightly.

Arjun lifted her face and saw tears streaming down her face.

He kissed her gently and pulled her closer.

"Can I stop you from leaving?" Disha asked amidst her tears.

That tugged at Arjun's heart.

"I am already finding it difficult to go, Disha," Arjun said.

Disha looked into Arjun, who is almost teary-eyed, and understood that she is not alone in this, and Arjun likes her too.

Arjun pulled her close and kissed her.

Disha kissed him back, and they continued until they moved and fell onto the bed.

Arjun looked into Disha's eyes and wiped her tears.

Disha hugged him tighter, unable to say anything to him. She knows he has to go, and she should not stop him. She understood Arjun doesn't know what to do at the moment; she shouldn't be questioning him and confusing him now.

"Shall we pack your stuff?" Disha asked, trying to keep a straight face.

"Don't you want to share what is on your mind?" Arjun asked.

"I am scared to ask. Maybe I don't want to know the answer," Disha replied.

"Then maybe I should answer the unasked questions?" Arjun replied.

Disha kissed him as if to stop.

Arjun kissed her back passionately until she was out of breath.

A Pact to Face Uncertainties

Then he said, "Do you know you look beautiful?"

Disha looked at him and said, "Is that even a topic of discussion?"

Arjun laughed and said, "That is what I like about you. You are very understanding yet naive. You are strong, yet I know your weakness. You love with all your heart, but still stop yourself if you are overwhelmed by others. There is so much to you that a few words are not enough. Whenever I am with you, I feel as if I have become stronger, and at the same time, I feel like I have to protect you. You confuse me many times. Your wavelength and thoughts match with most of mine. I love how you respond to me and how you make love. I feel like I am the only special one in your life, knowing fully well I am not."

Tears started rolling from Disha's eyes, and she stopped Arjun from saying anything further. She mustered up a lot of courage to let him go. Now, he is tugging at her heart. She wouldn't be able to stay rational if he continued. She wanted him to stay with her. She doesn't want him to go. She wants to have a family together, but she doesn't see a way forward.

Arjun bit her hand slightly as she stopped him. When she got angry and tried to pull herself away, he pulled her back and kissed her hand.

"Let me complete what I want to say, please?" asked Arjun.

"Mmm," said Disha.

He pulled her closer into his arms and said, "Disha, my sweetheart, I love you. I want to spend the rest of my life with you, but currently, I must go back to the US."

I do not know how long it will take me to settle things there. I will plan everything and will come back. I promise I will come back, and I will beg and plead with you to marry me. I am planning to take you, ma, and Ananya with me. I want to take care of all of you. I want to be doing all the things I want to do with my family. I missed out on a lot of being stupid these many years, and I don't want to waste any other moment. I love you like crazy, and I want to spend the rest of my life with you. I want to be able to protect my mum. I want to give her all the love I didn't. Right now, my career is going great, and I just can't give up everything and stay here. Please understand, my love," said Arjun.

"I understand, Arjun. I do, but that is something I am unable to do. I really don't want to give up everyone and go. I don't want to leave mum alone. I will not be sane without you around me. I hate long-distance relationships. You cannot know what the state of mind of the other person is. I will become more unhappy, and at the end of the day, no one will be happy, and I don't want to be the cause of your unhappiness," said Disha.

"Is this going to make me happy, Disha?" Arjun said with subtle anger popping up.

Tears welled up in Disha's eyes as she understood both sides, and it felt like a Catch-22.

"I don't want to lose him. I will go crazy without him, but I can't leave everyone for him. I don't want to give up on the rest of the world for Arjun. I feel a pain in my heart. I don't know what to do. I started to love my life, and everything seems to be beginning to break," thought Disha.

"Arjun, are we going to break up?" Disha asked, with tears streaming down her eyes.

Arjun turned around to see Disha crying. He got flustered, looking at her.

"No, no, no, no, baby, please don't cry. I am never leaving you in this lifetime. You are stuck with me. I will figure out a way for us. Please don't cry. I can't live without you, don't you know that, silly. You have cast your magic on me. I cannot get out of it, and I will never want to get out of it. I love you and Ananya a lot. I can't dare to lose you. I will figure this out. Please don't cry, baby." pleaded Arjun.

"But..." Disha tried to speak.

She suddenly remembered all the pain she went through with Varun ghosting her. He left her and went silent on her. She went numb for days and went through depression. It took her years to feel alive.

"If it happens again, I will die. I cannot take it again," Disha thought, and the tears continued to pour out.

"I am not going to go away and ghost you. Please don't go that route. I am never going to leave you, baby. You are my precious. I can never be away from you. I will figure out the way. Please don't cry," begged Arjun.

"Arjun, I love you, and I don't want to lose you," Disha said, sobbing.

"I was waiting to hear those words from you, and you say that crying." chided Arjun.

Disha rushed to Arjun and hugged him tightly. Arjun hugged her, planted a kiss on her head, and said, "You are mine, and I will never leave you. I will figure out a way, but you will need to give me time. You need to give us the time. I don't know the solution at the moment. Meanwhile, I don't want you to go into panic mode. I don't want you to connect your past experiences to the present. I don't want you to think that I will leave you alone or anything."

We will have lots of fights because we are two different people, and we will have our share of differences in opinion, but you should never panic about me leaving you. I love you too much to be able to live without you. I know we have been together only for a short time, but you have become the most important person in my life, and I will figure out how to do things.

For now, I will need to go back, and I need you to be okay about it. It is hard on me, too. I want to keep hugging you. I want to keep looking at those beautiful, mesmerising eyes. I want to keep making love to you. Gosh, you get on my

A Pact to Face Uncertainties

nerves in a beautiful way. It is going to kill me to be away from you, but you know, we need to be rational and practical about life. We need to understand the pros and cons. What works better for us, for our families, and most importantly, for Ananya? She needs to be a priority to us. She is our gift, and I know you have your concerns. I can promise to be the best dad ever, but you need to teach me and give me time to learn. I haven't been a dad before, you see."

"He is so perfect. He reads my mind as if it's his. I don't know what to do," thought Disha.

"Arjun, I am really scared," said Disha.

"Don't be. Main hoon naa," said Arjun in Shahrukh Khan's style, and Disha burst out laughing.

"Ah, that laugh," Arjun said, acting as if she was breaking his heart. She laughed even more.

Arjun packed his stuff, and they got ready for the flight.

"Goodbye for now," he said.

Goodbye, for now, a phrase so light but heavy to bear.

It is not forever, yet the heart aches as if you are letting go. It is like a door which is neither open nor completely closed. It is like an intermission in a movie, but without the timing clear. You don't know what is ahead, but you want to wait. If the first half of the movie is beautiful, then you wouldn't move an inch as you wouldn't want to miss it. In love, the intermission is a pain, for the time is filled with the memories so far and emotions about the unknown ahead.

Life doesn't always go as planned, and there are many ways to understand what happens. One thing is certain: you always have a choice. You can make decisions, but you also have to deal with the results. Sometimes, people who mean everything to you—like family or friends—suddenly leave your life. You may cry, feel lonely, and wish they would come back. But remember, your part in their life might be over. There's a saying, "God removes people from your life because he heard conversations you didn't hear." At the same time, new people can come into your life unexpectedly, making you feel like you've known them forever.

Disha bid her goodbye for now to Arjun and headed home. She dragged herself to her room, wondering what lies ahead.

CHAPTER 15

BECOMING EACH OTHER'S ROCK

Disha sat in her room, looking out of the window, thinking about the long wait ahead. She is so scared now that she is vulnerable, possibly in the same place again. She remembered the pain she went through when Varun went silent on her. The 22 hours of flight time is already killing her. She kept staring at the clock.

In the silent room and the quiet night,

I stay as I hear my breath.

Each tick of the clock resounds.

I wait for you to be found.

Missing you already,

The feeling starts to become real.

The agony is yet to start.

But it is all familiar.

I wonder where you are.

I dread if it is

Going to be another nightmare.

"Time will tell," they say.

But the heart doesn't stay.

A silent storm stretches in the brain.

bringing in turmoil in vain,

Oh, dear brain, you are so cruel.

Bring out the warmth, not the fuel.

Let me breathe and believe.

That this is going to be different.

Let me hold onto the promise of his return.

Please quieten the turmoil in you; let me hope.

He will come to me, and we will become one soon.

As Disha penned down her thoughts, she heard a beep. It was a message from Arjun. She smiled.

"Don't kill your brain with thoughts; the air hostess is beautiful, but you are in my heart ;)" it said.

"He's so cheesy," thought Disha and smiled.

ॐ Becoming Each Other's Rock ॐ

Arjun called her as soon as he landed. He knew she would be waiting. He assured her all was fine, and he would take some time to reach his room. His battery is almost dead, but not to worry.

Disha felt relieved. She finally felt like she is breathing again, while her worry is not unfounded, she felt maybe she is pushing Arjun to work too hard to lessen her worries. She thought that she needs to get a grip on herself.

Over the next couple of months, Arjun and Disha were constantly on the phone. They chatted day and night, sharing every single moment of their life. They learnt a lot about each other and missed each other even more.

Long-distance relationships have their own set of challenges, but Arjun and Disha's situation was more like a fear of losing each other. They are so scared to lose each other that they worked hard to understand each other.

Disha wondered many times what she would do without him. It is interesting, isn't it? Arjun was not in her life a few months ago, and now she is thinking about what she would do without him. Whether love makes you strong or weak is debatable. She is sure of one thing: she wants him in her life, but the scars from the past keep haunting her, not letting her move forward and trust. Varun's betrayal has caused her to question anyone who shows affection; she questions their commitment and wishes for them to leave her before it becomes too hard.

She is okay for the person to leave and questioned if the person stayed. She is broken so bad by that one person that she is finding it hard to believe the true love she is experiencing from Arjun. "Will he also leave me?" is the constant thought she has in her life.

Arjun had to break through her boundaries to help her out, and she would reach out and shower the love he longed for. Arjun started his day with her and ended it by telling her all the stories of the day. Anything he comes across, the first person he thinks of is Disha. He has been an open book to her and will always be. They thoroughly enjoyed their gossip, their long hours of chatting, and their calls.

He spoke to Gayatri and Disha's mum and understood her past better. He realised that Disha was holding on to Ananya as a lifeline, and had Ananya not come into her life, Disha would never have been the person she is now. He understood the anxiety Disha was feeling every moment he was away. He tried his best to make her feel the love rather than be afraid of pain. His pain lessened with her presence. She became his joy. She became his support, but occasionally, Disha had a meltdown after some silly fight. She feared him leaving her, and that fear made her lock herself away.

Arjun made sure to always be available to Disha. He ensured that she never waited for a response from him. Disha felt so relieved; her fears were calmed. She is not worried anymore. Arjun didn't move mountains or change his plans. He didn't

ஐ Becoming Each Other's Rock ௸

force her to change hers, but he ensured that her fears were addressed in the subtlest way possible.

Arjun loved every moment he spent with Disha. His life is filled with so many beautiful feelings. He doesn't feel alone or depressed anymore. He found a home in Disha. His guilt started to subside. He is now living a more fruitful life. His energy levels soared. He felt like a new man. He looked forward to everything. His day starts with Disha and ends with her.

Whenever Disha sounded low, Arjun would send her flowers. The flowers always had a hidden meaning. She smiled, and that was all he needed. She would click a picture of herself with the flowers and send it to him. He would then be reassured that she was okay. That is how they checked on each other. If she received the flowers and didn't respond, he would know she was still angry and would make her laugh through memes. He loved to see her smile, her giggles, and to pamper her. She is his lifeline, and he just could not lose love again.

Their bond grew stronger with each passing day. Arjun admired Disha's creativity and her ability to see beauty in the mundane. Disha was drawn to Arjun's intelligence and his unwavering support for her dreams. They began to rely on each other for advice, comfort and encouragement.

Through all that, I wish you were here became the constant theme of their discussion.

Disha pampered Arjun. She sent cute notes, showered him with gifts on the slightest occasions, and helped him with his work. They brainstormed ideas. It was like another world. They enjoyed and evolved together.

Arjun understood what she had never said. Isn't that what being in love is about? It might not just mean staying in the same place but being there.

One fine day, Arjun decided to surprise Disha, but then he remembered how freaked out Disha would get if she was unable to reach him. So, he avoided the surprise and told her he was going to come to India. He was working in the background and was creating a proposal, which required him to set up a team. He worked really hard to make sure that his proposal was approved, and it was finally done. Now, all he has to do is set up teams in India.

He shared it excitedly with Disha, and her joy knew no bounds. She started crying like anything, and his heart melted at the sight. He found true love.

As soon as he landed in India, Disha rushed and hugged him tightly. Her joy knew no bounds. She felt alive again. Arjun was also over the moon seeing Disha.

Arjun had to set up the team in other cities. So, he kept travelling between the cities, and Disha went along with him whenever he travelled. Their weekends were a blend of adventure and relaxation. From exploring the street food markets to attending music festivals, from quiet evenings, they made the most of what Mumbai had to offer.

Trips to other cities always require additional holiday planning.

Arjun met Disha's friends, who scrutinised him forever. He understood her world. He met Ananya and her mum. Ananya enjoyed Arjun's company, and she had so many questions. Arjun loved playing with her, and whenever he had time, he visited Ananya and picked her up sometimes from school. They had their own routine of going to the ice cream parlour and, later on, visiting her mum's place to pick her up and end up with dinner.

For Disha, this was a dream she never dared to dream of. She felt her family to be complete. She felt calm and looked forward to every single day. It felt too good to be true, but she found someone so right for her. She felt like, finally, I can let go of being strong. I found someone I could rely on.

Arjun was around for the next six months, and he never felt alive. He loved every moment he had with Disha. They enjoyed each other's company. The day started with "Good morning" and ended with long talks. Now they were able to sense each other's mood, they knew each other's likes and dislikes, and they knew each other's turn-ons too. Arjun drove Disha crazy, and Disha was no less. However, at the back of their minds, both had an unresolved situation about what was next. Arjun had to go back, and Disha didn't want to leave the country.

ॐ Fate Intertwined ☙

Despite their best efforts, Arjun and Disha faced setbacks in their personal and professional lives. Disha's mum had a heart attack and had to undergo surgery. Arjun was around supporting Disha all through. He was beside her, taking care of her, being her strength.

Arjun understood what Disha is feeling. He tried his best to be there. There were many times Disha broke down and just wanted him to leave her. He knew all she needs is reassurance that he won't leave her. Whenever she felt that, Arjun dropped everything and rushed to her. He hugged and pampered her, took her away, and did whatever made her feel better. He felt angry towards Varun for breaking her so bad. He would have killed him if he came across him again.

Disha always had that feeling in her mind that he might leave her. The closer they came, the more anxious she became. She thought of ways to cope if he leaves her. She would suddenly snap at him when he was away on work or when he could not meet her and melt right away when he came to her. She was a confused soul, and Arjun was confused even more, but Arjun knew better.

Arjun has his share of worries. He panicked every time Disha would get upset. He held her close every time they had to cross the road. He constantly checked on where she was. He is too afraid to lose her, and he does everything to make sure she is ok. Whenever she had to travel, Arjun joined her. The thought of leaving her and going back to the US is killing him already, and Disha's begging eyes don't help much, either. He is too worried, but then, when he thinks logically, he works hard for something, and he is almost there. He didn't want to give up now.

Arjun is deeply and madly in love with Disha, but he has his entire world in the US. He felt it would be better professionally and personally to stay in the US. He knew Disha loved him a lot, too. He grew fond of Ananya as well. He understood her world, and pulling her out of her comfort zone didn't seem like a good idea. She would feel lonely in the US. She is happy here, but she might feel out of place there. Arjun was not sure of what to do next. Disha understood his predicament and also encouraged him to go. She loved him dearly, and she respected him even more. He achieved a lot in such a short time. She cannot be the reason for him not to be fulfilling his goal. She loved him dearly, but that doesn't mean he has to change and give up his goals and dreams to stay with her. She cannot be deciding that for him.

Disha knew what Arjun wanted, but she was not ready to disturb the lives of Ananya and her mum.

Yes, she is madly in love with Arjun, but he is not her only world. She has her own world. She has her friends and her family, who mean a lot to her. She worked so hard to reach where she is, and giving up all for one person didn't feel right to her. Ten years ago, she would have done it without hesitation, but life taught her a very big lesson. Never make someone so important in your life that you feel nothing without them.

She remembered how Varun didn't even trust that she would be on his side and moved away without uttering a word. She felt that Varun didn't feel secure enough to share with her that his priorities were different. He left her crudely, hurting her more and literally damaging her. She cannot do that to Arjun. He should feel her support in his life. She cannot stop him nor be a blocker in his life. She needs to be able to support him, guide him, and be calm rather than chaos.

Their past helped them in many ways, especially in treating each other better, and they worked towards understanding each other. But at the same time, they understood that giving importance to oneself is also very critical. You need to respect yourself first.

Disha and Arjun talked through all the possible scenarios and discussed at length on what could be the best thing to do. The fact is, they love each other and want to spend their life together. While the reality is that they need to take time and understand how best to do it.

Disha needs to take care of her mum, and Ananya is not ready to move. Arjun's work is going great, and it will do wonders for his career. At this point, disrupting each other's life is a foolish thing to do. So, they decided to explore life as it is. They made commitments to each other and made plans to go around the world. They will carefully plan their vacations and make sure to make the best of the situation until they get to live together.

People tend project and expect the happy endings like in the movies onto your life. There is no happy ending if you are giving up yourself unless that is what you want. Love is about understanding each other and not about adjusting. You always get to choose the life you want.

Disha and Arjun understood it early in their life. It is important to cherish every single moment without losing oneself. They found strength in each other, as well as gained confidence in themselves. Coming across each other is definitely a blessing. They are perfect for each other. While they might not be together immediately, they can plan their life. Each one is working towards their own goal while supporting the other.

Their fears are overcome. Now, Disha is no longer afraid of losing someone to long-distance. She is not afraid to trust, and Arjun also doesn't feel as much guilt as before. He is still very cautious about surprises and is careful about Disha's travelling, but he has accepted that he cannot hold on to the past. He needs to let go and accept what life is offering.

CHAPTER 16

A LIFETIME OF LOVE

Two souls met when they were at their lowest,

Troubled by their past, and the future was unclear.

Only when they voiced it did they hear.

what their hearts wanted, and their fears

Together, they faced the shadows of the past.

Hand in hand, they hurried along.

Finding solace in the promises they kept.

They found the love they deserved the most.

Through the tears and laughter, their bond did grow.

They feared a lot, but they now know for sure.

They can let go, for they are pure.

Their journey was not always easy,

Fate Intertwined

But their love is unwavering,

Now, as they walk the path.

They know it in their heart.

Through tangled threads of time,

Their fate was intertwined.

Arjun and Disha have become each other's rock, a source of strength and comfort in an ever-changing world. Their story is a testament to the power of love, resilience, and the beauty of building a life together, even when you are apart.

Disha sat by her window, thinking about the past two years. When they decided to live in different countries to follow their dreams and fulfil their responsibilities, it was tough. They missed being together on special days, and the long-distance calls were hard. But these challenges only made their love stronger.

It wasn't hard for them to keep their relationship strong. They understood each other well. They found creative ways to stay in touch. They scheduled regular video calls, sent each other gifts, and even had virtual movie nights. These efforts helped them feel close, even when they were miles apart. They committed to life. They worked hard on their life goals. They went on many vacations, sometimes just the two of them and sometimes with both families. They made the best of every chance they got.

೫ A Lifetime of Love ೫

Love is a challenge in itself. Though it is a universal language, it is the most difficult one to comprehend. The major requirement for love to flourish is communication. Communication is for understanding, not for responding. These challenges, while difficult, made them stronger. They learnt to be resilient and patient, qualities that strengthened their bond.

"This is my person," is a thought that makes a lot of difference in how you treat each other.

There were times when the distance felt unbearable. Arjun had a setback when one of his major projects didn't turn out as planned. Disha lost her job due to layoffs. During these tough times, they leaned on each other for support. Late-night calls and heartfelt messages helped them through their darkest moments.

Disha decided to use the time to build a startup. She always had a vision towards making life simple. She took time to understand the nuances of building a startup. She decided to build a data analytics app that provides healthcare solutions. She built the use cases and worked out the details of challenges in a healthcare institution. She read a lot about how the healthcare system collapsed during Covid and what is needed. She felt extremely motivated to do something. What started as a pet project took a serious turn. Arjun and Disha spent hours building the nuances of the solution. They decided to create a solution for elderly care support. They worked on the virtual care support options that provided a series of solutions catering to the different needs of elderly people living alone.

They finally decided to start a company together. They detailed the plan. Arjun continued to work, and Disha crafted the details of how the company should run. They became very excited about what lay ahead. They are going to build on their dreams of being together and also building their own company.

Arjun and Disha realised that true love is not just about the happy moments but about standing by each other through thick and thin. They had found in each other a partner, a friend, and a soulmate. Their journey so far is a beautiful reminder that love when nurtured with care and commitment, can withstand any challenge and become the foundation of a fulfilling life together.

They finally decided to tie the knot. Their reunion was everything they had hoped for. Their love was stronger than ever. They had learnt to balance their individual goals with their relationship, creating a partnership that was both supportive and fulfilling. They spent evenings cooking together, discussing their days, and planning their future. The time apart had taught them the value of patience and understanding.

Fate always gives you choices, and the choice you make decides the life you will lead. Disha and Arjun's story was one of love, resilience, and growth. They had proven that with dedication and support, it was possible to achieve their dreams without losing each other. Their hearts were united, even when their paths had been separate, and that was the true strength of their love.

Their fate has finally intertwined.

AFTERWORD AND ADDITIONAL INSIGHTS

First and foremost, I would like to extend my deepest gratitude to the readers who have embarked on this journey with me. Your support and enthusiasm have been invaluable. To my family and friends, thank you for your unwavering encouragement and patience as I poured my thoughts into this story.

"Fate Intertwined" is a testament to the belief that love can find us in the most unexpected places and times. This story explores the themes of destiny, resilience, and the enduring power of love. I hope it has touched your heart and provided a glimpse into the beautiful chaos that love can bring into our lives. Writing this book has been a journey of reflection and discovery, and I am grateful for the opportunity to share it with you.

Milton Keynes UK
Ingram Content Group UK Ltd.
UKHW031206251124
451566UK00004B/11